THE LAST RESORT

OLD SCHOOL MYSTERIES
BOOK 4

ANDREA C. NEIL

Sign up for the AceWrites Newsletter to receive exclusive content and more: acneil.com/newsletter

For Dayl, Russ, and Hallie - Mahalo

CHAPTER 1

Delphine Lougheed lay in a lounge chair next to the salt-water pool of the exclusive Club at Kaimoa Bay, watching her friend Kenji Yamamoto check around their poolside encampment for his laptop. He riffled through his messenger bag, looked under his chair, and went back to the messenger bag again.

"You really should keep better track of that thing," Delphine said.

Kenji dropped his arms to his sides and gave her a face he rarely used—complete and utter vexation. She felt only a tiny bit bad about annoying him. It served him right for bringing a laptop on a Hawaiian vacation in the first place.

"I only went to buy Marge a candy bar. I do not understand where it could have gone," he said.

"It's not your work laptop, is it?" she asked him.

His silence provided her with the answer.

"Oh dear," she said.

Delphine and Kenji were retired spies, in the sense that neither of them claimed full-time status with the international shadow agency who'd employed them for decades. However, Delphine had gotten pulled into a few agency embroilments recently, and she'd discovered Kenji still "consulted" for them from time to time. You never really got out.

But today, Delphine was on a real vacation. Not the stay-at-home kind; not the kind where someone came to visit her in Pasadena and she had to show them around Los Angeles; not the sort where she went to visit family in Oklahoma for Christmas. This vacation consisted of six days relaxing on the small Hawaiian island of Mokumoa. Her only objective for the foreseeable future was to rest and enjoy some much needed and well-deserved time to herself.

When Delphine had first conceived of the idea to visit Mokumoa, she'd wanted to travel alone. But her friend and fellow grandma Marge Flanders had been staying with her for a little over a month, with no signs of seeking a more permanent residence somewhere else. And why would Marge want to, when her new boyfriend, Kenji, lived right across the street from Delphine? Kenji was Delphine's very best friend. They were thick as thieves, and in their case, the phrase held a kernel of truth. But these days he seemed to spend most of his energy making googly-eyes at Marge. Which was fine, but Delphine wished the two of them didn't have to be so googly in front of her all the time. She missed her privacy.

Even after considering all the angles, Delphine hadn't been able to find a way to run off to Hawaii without telling her friends. Trying to keep a secret from her roommate was about as useless as a treadmill for a fish, or whatever kind of thing Marge liked to say. Goodness, thought Delphine, now she was starting to sound like Marge. Disconcerting, to say the least.

In the end, Delphine hadn't wanted to insult her friends by excluding them, so she'd taken the high road and invited them along.

Ostensibly, they were all there to visit Delphine and Marge's granddaughter Griffin Beckett, who had started her new job on the beautiful tropical island a few weeks earlier. Delphine had thought it might be nice to support Griffin, and if their familial encouragement happened to take the form of a Hawaiian vacation, so be it.

The Kaimoa Bay Club and its neighboring resort were owned by the famous film director Fausto Conte—an old friend of Delphine's, whom she had asked to provide employment for Griffin. After Delphine assured Fausto that yes, she now "owed him one," he'd found a position for her granddaughter, working with one of his estate managers on Mokumoa. Fausto owned the club, resort, and a large family compound, which bordered one side of the club. He might own other properties on the island too, and perhaps some cacao and coffee farms.

Finding work for Griffin had been the least Delphine could do after causing her granddaughter to lose her job as a forensic accountant with the FBI. At the time, Delphine felt the FBI wasn't challenging enough for the incredibly bright young woman, yet assertiveness had never been one of Griffin's strong suits, and she never sought out new opportunities on her own. So Delphine pulled a few strings, and whoopsie! Griffin got laid off.

Soon after losing her job, however, Griffin's husband Brian left her for their real estate agent. Delphine had learned her lesson: Only meddle in the employment history of your family when you were certain your plan wouldn't get derailed by some other area of life at the same time. Which basically meant, never meddle in the employment history of your family.

But now Griffin was divorced, reemployed, and hopefully enjoying her new start. The job wasn't in accounting, Griffin's chosen field, but it was something, and it would have to do for now. Griffin worked with Fausto's head of security, who oversaw all the Conte properties. Apparently, they spent a lot of time running errands and taking care of odd jobs. It was a place to start though, and Delphine knew if Fausto was smart, in time he'd move her brilliant granddaughter into a position that might suit everyone better.

Delphine, Kenji, and Marge had arrived on Mokumoa that morning and had only been at the resort a few hours, but already

Delphine had started to feel more relaxed. After her stint in Miami rescuing Marge from a ring of senior jewel thieves, followed closely by trying to clear her own name in a nefarious cheese-smuggling plot, and then having to locate Marge's shady ex-boyfriend after he kidnapped himself at Disneyland, Delphine wanted, quite simply, quiet and rest. Less danger would be nice too. As would not having to save other people all the time. Yes, this vacation would work out perfectly, as long as she could keep Kenji and Marge out of her hair. But that should be doable. Right? Now, if they could just find Kenji's laptop, she could get back to lounging. But the specter of derailed plans hung over her like a tropical-storm raincloud.

"You aren't messing with me, are you? Do you have my laptop?" Kenji asked. He eyed her tote bag, which hung from the back of her chair.

"Why on earth would I do that?" asked Delphine. "I want as little excitement as possible for the next five days." She sat up. "How could you lose it?"

Kenji searched through his own bag for the third time, not saying anything.

"Lose what?" said Marge as she appeared next to Delphine's chair.

"Everything is fine," said Kenji in a tight voice. He wandered over to an umbrella-shaded patio table near their lounge chairs. He'd sat there earlier, checking his email. Now he picked up another wet towel that had been lying on a chair and looked under the table. And up at the shade umbrella.

Marge plopped down on the chaise longue next to Delphine's. She shook her head to get pool water out of her short, white hair and sprayed Delphine in a not-so-fine mist for the third time that afternoon. Delphine retrieved her extra towel and dried herself off. Again.

"He's misplaced his laptop," Delphine said.

Kenji made a disapproving snort.

"He lost it?" asked Marge. "When we were packing, I told

him, why bring a dumb ol' laptop on vacation in the first place? Didn't I tell you, Kenji? But did you listen? Noooooo."

Kenji grumbled something Delphine couldn't hear.

"You're really stressed about it?" Marge asked him.

"It was … expensive," said Kenji, flicking his gaze to Delphine, who pretended not to notice.

Marge sighed loud enough for people in the pool to hear. "You can stop looking, K-Man, I have it." She reached under her chair and picked up her canvas tote bag. She pulled out the laptop and held it out to him.

Kenji ran over to her and snatched it up, hugging it to his chest.

"Sheesh," said Marge. "I just wanted to keep it safe for you."

"Thank you," said Kenji in a not-very-thankful-sounding tone.

"I didn't want it to get stolen," Marge explained.

"Yes Kenji, think of what might happen if it got stolen," said Delphine.

CHAPTER 2

Marge felt bad she'd made Kenji stressed out by taking his laptop. She'd only wanted to keep it safe! Okay, maybe there had been a little more to it. He seemed to be on it so much that sometimes she got a little jealous. And on a Hawaiian vacation? Come on, who needed a laptop on a vacation. Especially when things were heating up in their relationship. This trip away was a big step for them. She felt a little nervous about it, to be honest.

"When do we get to see Griffy?" Marge asked as she settled into her lounge chair. It was late in the afternoon and their chairs were shaded by some short palm trees, so no catching any more rays today. But at their age, they probably didn't need to be out in the sun much anymore anyway.

Delphine put her sunglasses back on after wiping them off with a towel. "I got a text from her a little while ago. She's going to join us for dinner tonight."

"I can't wait to hear how much she likes her new job!" said Marge.

Delphine said, "I hope she likes it."

"What's not to like? Look at this place." Marge pointed to the bay, just beyond the club's patio area and private stretch of beach.

The water shone like some sort of blue gemstone collection; sparkly and clear and breathtaking. Like a handful of diamonds.

"There is probably something not to love about this place," said Kenji from his chair, where he was slathering himself with SPF100 lotion. "But I cannot think of what it might be."

As if in response to his words, a big gust of wind came up out of nowhere. It wasn't a warm breeze either; it had a chill to it, and it brought goosebumps to Marge's skin. A lone cloud whizzed in front of the cheerful South Pacific sun and placed the patio area in a nest of darkness. Five seconds later, the breeze disappeared, and the cloud moved on.

"That was weird," said Marge, looking up at the sky.

"For sure," said Kenji, also gazing skyward. "And creepy."

"It's like the beginning of one of those artsy movies, where they use some kind of weird weather or natural disaster or whatever to foreshadow something omnivorous to come," said Marge.

"Don't you mean ominous?" asked Delphine.

"What? No, I don't think so," said Marge.

Kenji's phone pinged and he read the screen. "I got a text confirming our paddleboard lessons for tomorrow. Miko has set it up."

Marge clapped her hands. "Yippee! Paddling around on a floaty thing sounds like so much fun."

"Thank you, Delphine, for arranging it for us," said Kenji.

"It's my pleasure," said Delphine. "How fortunate that Griffin's colleague is so well connected. I'm sure he can arrange all sorts of fun adventures for you two."

"Don't you want to come on some adventures?" asked Marge.

Delphine picked at her towel. "Of course. But I think you two should have some time alone."

Kenji put his phone down and scrutinized her. "Are you feeling okay?"

"Don't be ridiculous, of course I'm okay. I'd rather just relax."

"Hmm," said Kenji.

Marge said, "Kenji, leave her be. She's a little older than we are, so she's probably slowing down is all. You know, approaching her dotage or whatever."

"I'll have you know Kenji is the oldest of the three of us," said Delphine.

"No problemo, Big D," said Marge, winking at her.

Delphine scowled. "Do you have to talk to me like I'm your plumber?"

Marge crossed her arms and tried to hold back a smile.

"Remember we are all on the same team here," said Kenji, sounding a little alarmed.

Poor fella, thought Marge. It always stressed him out when she and Delphine went at it; he always tried so hard to keep the peace. But there was never any real malice behind the arguments, and Marge suspected Delphine enjoyed their lively conversations as much as she did.

"All good, Mega Boyfriend," said Marge.

A few minutes went by in silence as they watched a very beautiful woman in a sari and tiny bikini top serve pink fruity drinks to a nearby couple.

"Those look yummy," said Marge.

"Yes they do," said Kenji, who observed the young lady walk away. Marge hit him with her wet towel.

"Did you tell her yet?" Kenji asked Marge.

"Tell me what?" said Delphine.

Marge unwrapped her candy bar and took a big bite. She felt a lump form in her throat, and not just from the peanuty, nougaty snack she'd bitten into. She rolled her head to the right to glance at Kenji, who gave her a nod of encouragement.

"So what is it?" Delphine said. "The suspense is—"

"Killing you?" said Kenji.

"Annoying."

Marge swallowed her snack and sat up and faced Delphine, who also sat up. "Well, see, here's the thing, Big D..." But she couldn't go on; the words wouldn't come.

Delphine sat there staring at her. Impatience rolled off her in waves. Not helping!

Marge furrowed her brow in concentration. "Okay. Well. I know I said I'd be your roommate and stuff, but … Kenji and I have talked about it, and we decided we want to spend more time together. You know, at night. And in the morning. And basically all the time. So, um, I'm gonna stay with him in his room."

"Oh," said Delphine. Her face showed no trace of emotion. "Okay."

"What? That's all you have to say?" asked Marge.

"We're all in our seventies here," said Delphine.

"Do you always have to remind us we're old?" snapped Marge.

"You didn't let me finish," said Delphine. "I meant we're all adults who have been around the proverbial block a few times. And you two have been seeing each other a little while now. It's only natural you want to be together in such a romantic place."

"Hmm," said Marge, somewhat suspicious of Delphine's good mood.

"She said she is fine," Kenji said, trying to assure her.

But Marge didn't know about his motives either. What if he was trying to make everything seem okay for the sole purpose of getting into her undies? They hadn't taken the physical side of their relationship very far yet, but now they were about to share a room, and the big event felt imminent. Or inevitable. Or like a sure thing. However you were supposed to put it.

"I don't want Delphine to be lonely though," said Marge. "You know how she relies on us for companionship."

"You don't believe me when I say I'll be fine?" asked Delphine. "Oh, I see. I should be sadder. Very well. Marge, please don't leave me, I'll be all alone and so bored and unhappy without you." She interlaced her fingers together and brought the knuckles to the bottom of her chin. She even gave Marge puppy-dog eyes.

Marge looked at Kenji and said, "I don't feel bad anymore."

Delphine stood and hung her purse from her shoulder. "Come on, Marge. Let's go to the bar. I'll buy you one of those fruity drinks you like."

"Fine," said Marge. "But only because I'm thirsty, and not because I can be bought."

"I love that you are so feisty," Kenji whispered.

"You ain't seen nothing yet, K-Man," she whispered back. She put her swimsuit cover-up over one arm and stood to give Kenji a kiss.

CHAPTER 3

Delphine and Marge said goodbye to Kenji and began to make their way across the club patio. It was a Saturday afternoon, and the club was quite crowded. Delphine marveled at the luxury of the place, which came at them from all sides.

The large open space featured a beautiful saltwater pool and Jacuzzi, an outdoor bar, and a wide sandy path led to a private beach. Other paths went to the adjacent luxury hotel, a few tennis and pickleball courts, and a state-of-the-art health club. A deck for outdoor seating of the club's award-winning restaurant overlooked everything.

And the guests! Everyone seemed so handsome and healthy. Granted, she, Marge, and Kenji were probably some of the oldest patrons, but Delphine didn't feel out of place.

"Is that a CougarWear cover-up?" Delphine asked, pointing to the flimsy garment draped over Marge's arm. The leopard-print fabric was thin, yet sturdy, and matched Marge's swim skirt. The garments made Delphine think of when she had searched the CougarWear warehouse space in Cypress a month earlier. The company, owned by one Buffy van Cougar, made swimsuits and other athleisure items for the post-menopausal population. The shelves in the work room had been lined with bolts of fabric in bright colors and garish designs.

"I was hoping you wouldn't notice," said Marge. "I know how you feel about CougarWear. And its owner."

"It wasn't *my* boyfriend who two-timed me with Buffy van Cougar," said Delphine.

"Yeah yeah," said Marge, sounding like she'd rather forget about her ex-boyfriend Willard and his cheating ways. Fair enough.

Delphine patted Marge on the shoulder. "I'm just surprised; all things considered. And even though Frances Flance is suing them for terrible quality issues, doesn't mean you can't still try your luck with the stuff." Frances was Delphine's long-time friend and an ace attorney who'd had a little mishap with a CougarWear swimsuit in the Disneyland Hotel swimming pool a month earlier. Frances was not someone you'd want to be in litigation with, so Delphine didn't have high hopes for the survival of the swimwear company.

Marge smoothed the fabric of her neon-pink tankini. "No offense to your friend, but she's kind of built like a freight train. Maybe Buffy's clothing is made for a more … refined kind of gal."

Delphine was about to let out a snappy comeback, but Marge's attention had been directed elsewhere. She seemed to be staring at someone seated at the bar. She slowed down and came to a stop.

"Are you all right?" asked Delphine.

Marge was ogling a man. Delphine took a closer look at him. It was Brock Celery, one of the most famous celebrities of their generation.

"Oh. My. Stars," said Marge. "B… Br… Brock."

"Oh my," said Delphine.

Delphine didn't usually fawn over movie stars, having met many over the years. They were often self-centered, too focused on appearance, and occasionally short on working brain synapses. But Brock Celery was an exception. He had it all: looks, intelligence, and charm. Also money, if she were being thorough in her assessment. They'd met a long time ago; she wondered if he remembered her.

Marge tossed her cover-up into the air, yelled "Aaaaauuuuuuooooo!" and took off at a sprint for the bar.

The outburst had been so loud Delphine jumped in surprise, and the noise sent her nervous system into fight-or-flight mode. Without meaning to, she immediately reverted to spy mode, and it took all her restraint not to drop to the ground and roll a few times to dodge imaginary bullets. She'd been retired for a while, but she'd never be able to let go of old tendencies. They were too ingrained by now.

Delphine watched Marge travel at alarming speed toward Brock Celery and decided it might be a good idea to follow her, in case Marge did something Delphine would need to apologize for later. She, Marge, and Kenji had paid for their rooms themselves, but they were still personal guests of Mr. Conte, and as such Delphine felt they should at least attempt to retain a certain level of decorum. She'd forgotten to mention the suggestion to Marge though.

By the time Delphine caught up with Marge, Marge had joined a group of four other women standing in a semicircle around Brock's barstool. The shirtless movie star gave his admirers a blinding smile and lifted his glass. He seemed a little too old to go shirtless, in Delphine's opinion, but she may have been more modest than most. His physique wasn't too bad for his age, but his leathery skin betrayed evidence of too much time spent in the sun.

As he sucked some of his green tropical drink through his straw, he raised one eyebrow at his admirers in a provocative gesture.

"Ooooooh," said several of the ladies, none of whom appeared to be under the age of sixty. One of them turned red and looked like she might be having a hot flash.

Brock's first major blockbuster film had been *Stop That Milkwagon!* in the early '70s. Delphine remembered the movie well. She had been a young impressionable woman—just the demographic a Brock Celery movie targeted back then.

"Delphine!" Brock waved at her where she stood behind his gaggle of admirers. "What a delight to see you here."

The five women surrounding him slowly turned in her direction. They stared at her with so much disdain she began to question her own existence.

"Oh, hello Brock," she said, and gave him a finger wave.

"Come on now, get over here and give me a hug." Brock stood from his stool and opened his arms wide.

The women parted like the Red Sea to make way for her, and she walked up to Brock but only stuck out her hand, which he shook with reluctance. No way would she hug a sweaty shirtless film icon in front of a group of jealous women. Especially when one of those women was Marge. Delphine would never hear the end of it. Ever.

"Hello, Brock," said Delphine. "It's good to see you again."

Someone cleared their throat to her left. Marge had stepped up to join her.

Brock dazzled the two of them with his signature smile. "Well hello, who's this?" He eyed Marge in her pink and leopard-print swimsuit.

"Hiiiiiii," said Marge, sounding like a lovestruck teenager. She began to lean on Delphine, but her eyes never left Brock Celery. Delphine tried to prop her up, but Marge was heavier than she appeared.

Brock smiled at Marge. "Hi."

If Delphine didn't know better, she would've said Marge had lost her ability to speak in full sentences. Delphine hadn't known her friend was such a Brock fan, but then again, they didn't share much idle chitchat about crushes.

"Brock, this is my friend Marge Flanders," said Delphine.

"Hi there, Marge," said Brock.

"Hiiiiiii," said Marge. She stepped forward and opened her arms as if to give him a hug, but in response, he held out his hand for her to shake, and she took it, not quite happy with her consolation prize. No shirtless-movie-star hugs for her.

"I'll just order you and your boyfriend some drinks, shall I?" Delphine asked Marge.

"Okay," said Marge, still not looking at her.

Delphine shook her head at her friend and flagged down the bartender. "Three Pellegrinos, please. With lime." The last thing Marge needed was an inhibition-loosening alcoholic drink.

"I love your movies, Mr. Celery," said Marge in a dreamy voice. She sat down on the stool next to Brock, to the dismay of the other women, who were watching Marge for signs of weakness. Like a pride of lions, Delphine thought.

Brock's eyes swung to Delphine's, and he winked at her. "Oh yeah?"

"Uh-huh," said Marge. "I'm your biggest Celery Stalker."

"What is a Celery Stalker?" asked Delphine. She stood in front of the two stools with her back to the lions.

"My fans are called Celery Stalkers," said Brock. "Came up with it myself." This time he winked at Marge, who let out a tiny moan in response.

"You like having stalkers, do you?" Delphine wondered what it said about the man.

"It's all for fun," he said with a wave of his hand.

"I'm in the official club and everything," said Marge.

"Well that's great, babe," said Brock Celery. "Say, what are you doing la—"

"Brock, it's time to go, you've got a phone interview in five." A young man, who must've been Brock's manager or publicist, pushed his way in front of Delphine. She stepped back to join the outer circle of fans, bumping into a woman wearing a one-piece bathing suit with a plunging neckline.

"Watch it, sister," growled the woman as she fanned her décolletage.

The young man addressed the lions. "Sorry ladies, Brock's got to go. Let's give the man some space, okay? Remember, he's here to relax."

"I hope you have a nice relaxing, uh, relax," Marge said to Brock, who laughed.

"Biff, please make sure this young lady here gets one of our official Celery Stalker trucker hats. And a sticker." Brock Celery stood up to leave.

"Wait!" said Marge. "Would you sign my swimsuit?"

A lascivious grin spread across Brock Celery's face and Delphine thought she might pass out with embarrassment.

"Anyone got a pen?" he asked loudly.

Biff shook his head. Marge gave Delphine a hopeful look.

Of course Delphine had a pen, but there was no way in hell Brock Celery would get it. "Sorry, no," Delphine told Marge.

Brock stared at Marge's pink tankini. "What a shame," he said. "Babe, next time I see you, I'll sign whatever you want me to, okay?"

Marge's eyes glazed over. "'Kay."

Brock and Biff left the bar, and the other ladies wandered off since the Brock show had officially ended.

"Sign my swimsuit?" said Delphine. "What are you, fifteen?"

"Oh get over it, Miss I-know-tons-of-famous-people," griped Marge. Suddenly she jumped. "Oh no! He doesn't have my address to send me a hat!"

"How devastating," said Delphine.

Marge's face softened. "He called me babe."

"Yes, but Kenji calls you Super Babe," said Delphine.

"Kenji who?"

Delphine helped Marge stand up from her stool. "Come on, let's go. Carry these waters." She handed two glasses to Marge.

"Water?" said Marge.

"You're in no shape to drink anything stronger."

Delphine wondered if Brock Celery might throw a wrench in Kenji and Marge's relationship. Which could result in something even worse—the ruination of her own perfect vacation plans.

CHAPTER 4

It had taken herculean effort, but after reminding Marge of her boyfriend's last name a few times, Delphine eventually convinced her friend they should go back to the pool and rejoin Kenji.

When they got there, Marge and Kenji decided to go swimming again. Delphine settled back onto her chaise longue, eyes closed, grateful for a few solitary moments. In a lull between pool splashes, a muted conversation floated by on the breeze and caught her attention.

The patio area was filled with people. Club members and guests of the adjoining Kaimoa Bay Resort who had opted to purchase a club membership for the duration of their stay—for a considerable sum—sat around the pool and bar and moved through the area on their way to and from the beach. A resort such as this one, exclusive and expensive, tended to draw visitors from all over the world. But it wasn't often Delphine heard Norwegian spoken in public.

Delphine listened more closely. Somewhere behind her, a man and woman talked in hushed tones; not arguing but not enjoying a cheery conversation either. At one point it sounded like one of them mentioned *The Godfather* and cannoli. She picked out a few Norwegian words she recognized: *fisk, ananas,* and *gamall njósnari*.

The words translated as *fish, pineapple,* and... She couldn't be certain about the last one. It was either something about either the mafia or a surfboard. Funny how she still remembered the language after all these years. But it wasn't, not really. She remembered a lot from her long career. For example, she still knew how to say "put down your weapon" in Māori.

Before she could stop it, memories of her past life rushed in. During her decades-long career with the global shadow agency the Falls, she'd gone to Norway multiple times for various types of covert operations. Most people would be surprised at the number of unsavory activities that took place in the cold, beautiful country. She and Kenji had probably spent more time there than in any other country they'd worked in. Except maybe for several spots in South America. They'd worked in a lot of different places after all.

Most of their Norwegian missions had gone well ... a few had not.

The familiar cadence of the language drew her into a scene from their last trip to Norway. She had been in charge of a mission to uncover the true identity of the Fish Boss, the name they'd given to the don of the Herring Mafia, and take him out. The Herring Mafia was a particularly nasty group of Norwegians who controlled the Atlantic herring black market. They recruited a lot of members from the northern region of the country, the coldest places. Delphine shivered in the warm Hawaiian breeze.

The Falls had sent Delphine and her crew to hang out in Narvik for a few weeks, as rumor had it the Fish Boss was to visit, to personally oversee selecting a new capo and crew for the family. Kenji and Delphine had gotten stuck there for weeks. The whole unfortunate trip had culminated in a shootout in the produce section of the Bunnpris & Gourmet Narvik grocery store on Bolagsgata. Both sides sustained casualties, and to this day Delphine still couldn't bring herself to eat pickled herring.

Delphine braced herself and resolved to refocus on the present —she was in a tropical paradise after all, not a Norwegian supermarket. But these days it seemed everywhere she turned she came face to face with things that reminded her of her past. She'd felt so vital and alive as a spy. However, retirement was supposed to be a time to let those things go, to step out of the fray and make room for the younger generation. Or at least for those in better shape.

Marge and Kenji came back from the pool and picked up their towels. Marge got Delphine wet again as she dried off. Delphine gave up on rest.

As she sat up and reached for her towel, she chanced a glance over her shoulder to get a peek at whoever had been speaking Norwegian. She made out two figures sitting at a table but couldn't see any other details.

Kenji stuck a finger in his left ear, tilted his head to the left, and jumped up and down a few times.

"Still get water in your ears?" Delphine asked.

"Ever since the submarine incident." Marge stared at him, open-mouthed. "I mean the Disneyland submarine," he explained to her. "The pressure change was intense when we resurfaced."

Marge seemed satisfied with the answer and went to work searching for snacks in her tote bag.

Delphine remembered the submarine fiasco off the coast of Uruguay. They'd had to evacuate their ship when it got intercepted, and…

"K-Man, for Cripes' sake, what are you doing on your computer again?" asked Marge.

Kenji sat at the table with his laptop open and his fingers poised over the keyboard. His guilty gaze floated up to Marge, who stood nearby glaring at him with her hands on her hips.

"I am sorry, but I have a little bit of work to do."

"I thought you were retired, like the rest of us," said Marge. She tried to peek at Kenji's screen, but he closed the laptop as she approached.

Kenji pushed his reading glasses farther up his nose. "I do a little bit of consulting. With databases and informational systems and whatnot."

"Sounds boring," said Marge.

"It is," he said.

"Is it like, top secret stuff? Didn't you say one time you and Delphine used to do consulting together?"

Delphine's blood pressure rose. What on earth had Kenji told his girlfriend? Delphine thought they'd agreed not to share too much with Marge. For her safety as well as their own.

"A long time ago," said Kenji.

"Is that how you tracked Griffy's luggage when the airline lost it a few weeks back?"

"Yes," said Kenji. "I used the Air Suitcase Security program."

Marge cackled. "The ASS?"

Kenji scratched his head. "The what?" He shot Delphine a helpless expression.

Marge doubled over with laughter and slapped her thigh. "The ASS! You found her luggage in your—"

"Yes, well, I think we get it," said Delphine. She popped up out of her chair and pulled Marge away from the table.

"Ohhh," said Kenji. "I get it! A butt joke!" He opened his laptop again. "I never noticed it before."

"If I had a dollar for every terrible TLA we've run across over the years, I'd be a lot richer," said Delphine. Once again, she stole a glance in the direction from which she'd heard the Norwegian conversation earlier, but no one was there.

"What is a TLA?" asked Marge.

"A three-letter acronym," said Kenji in a kind tone.

"You people are weird," mumbled Marge.

Delphine took her time surveying the patio area as she stood there, and while she saw no one speaking Norwegian, something else caught her attention. Actually, it was a someone else.

On the other side of the pool stood a lone figure, leaning against a lamppost and staring right at her. He was a small man;

perhaps a bit taller than Delphine's height, which made it to 5'6" on a good day. He looked to be somewhere in his seventies.

He wore a faded black T-shirt and chino shorts. Medium-length gray hair stuck out from underneath a Dodger-blue bucket hat, complete with the LA Dodgers logo stitched in white. He'd pulled the small brim of the hat down so far it almost covered his eyes. He might have been of Hawaiian descent; Delphine couldn't be sure. His feet were bare, and his teeth were unusually white.

The man lifted one hand as a greeting. Without thinking too hard about it, she raised her hand in response. He grinned, turned, and disappeared into the crowd near the bar.

"It's just that you never told me you were working," Marge was saying to Kenji.

Delphine shook off the surprise at the strange encounter with the Dodger fan and rejoined the conversation. "There are probably all kinds of things your boyfriend hasn't told you," said Delphine.

"What's that supposed to mean?" Marge glared at Delphine.

"Yes, you are not helping," Kenji told Delphine. "Please stop."

Perhaps it had been an unfair thing to say, and she'd done it to stir up trouble. Maybe she felt grumpy because wasn't getting any alone time at the pool. Maybe she was irked she hadn't seen who'd been speaking Norwegian. Or perhaps the strange man in the Dodgers hat had thrown her off balance.

But really, why get bent out of shape by anything? She was on vacation! And who cared if someone spoke Norwegian in an internationally famous resort?

Well, Delphine did. Nothing about the event seemed unusual, yet she felt uneasy. By this point in her life, she'd learned to trust her intuition, but sometimes it didn't always come through loud and clear. She wondered what it was trying to tell her now.

CHAPTER 5

"I have an idea," said Delphine as she sat back down on her lounge chair.

"I am not sure I want to hear any of your suggestions right now," said Kenji, putting his laptop away.

"You'll like this one, I promise." Delphine took Marge by the arm. "Why don't the two of you go move your things into Kenji's room? Then it'll really feel like your romantic vacation has begun."

Marge looked at Kenji. "I guess that does sound like a good idea. Whaddya say, K-Man?"

"I think it is a great idea, Super Babe," said Kenji.

"Terrific," said Delphine. "I'll help you pack up your pool things." She picked up a folded towel, unfolded it and refolded it, and put it down again while Marge gathered her tote bag and SPF lotion.

"Kenji, could I please borrow your laptop? I'd like to do some research on icebergs." Delphine made sure to catch his eye, to double-check he'd understood her intent. Whenever one of them needed something important but didn't want anyone else to understand, they used a code word. Years ago, they'd chosen "iceberg." It seemed apropos, since many times in their line of work, things appeared small at first but often had huge unseen repercussions waiting right under the surface.

"Oh yes, of course," said Kenji. He reopened his laptop and typed in his twenty-one-digit password. Delphine knew it by heart, but she appreciated the gesture.

"Thank you," she said.

Marge, who either hadn't heard or didn't care that Delphine had felt the urge to research icebergs, swung her bag over her shoulder. "Let's go get this party started, if you know what I mean!"

Kenji rubbed his hands together. "Oh, I know what you mean!"

Delphine grimaced. "Bye-bye you two. Kenji, I'll drop your laptop by later, if you're not too busy starting your party."

Marge and Kenji left, and Delphine sat down at the table in front of the laptop. She glanced around the outdoor space; the strange barefoot man hadn't reappeared. For all she knew the Norwegian speakers were still in the pool area somewhere, since she had no idea what they looked like.

But that was about to change.

Her intuition kindly suggested she poke around a little bit. Something didn't sit right with her about the snippets of Norwegian she'd heard. Not that she could pinpoint what it had been. In any case, something compelled her to find out who the two people were.

Kenji's lock screen photo was a picture of him and Marge at the Huntington Library; Delphine had taken it herself a few weeks earlier when they invited her to attend high tea in the rose garden. It was a cute picture; they both seemed so happy. It made Delphine smile.

With a few swipes on the computer's trackpad, she navigated to one of the more unique programs Kenji had access to (TLA: BRP). A few more taps provided entry into the system which, when connected to another online service, allowed her to hack into the resort's security video camera feed.

Five minutes later she'd found the feed for the club pool. She chose a block of video from two hours earlier. Unfortunately, the resort only had one camera in the area. Based on the angle of the footage, the device must have been located on a pole near the bar. It featured a view of both the bar and the pool. Still, she was hopeful it would provide her a glimpse of the mystery Norwegians.

She skipped ahead to one hour earlier. But all she saw was a dark rectangle instead of an image of the club. The video appeared to have been shot in a pitch-black cave.

She skipped back a half hour from that point, and the video looked fine again. In the lower right corner sat Delphine in her lounge chair, and Marge and Kenji splashed around in the pool. Delphine fast-forwarded the footage until she got to the part where she and Marge were about to leave Kenji to get drinks at the bar. She watched as Marge stopped in her tracks, tossed her CougarWear swim cover-up into the air ... and the screen went black.

A groan of frustration left Delphine's lips. She got up from her chair and walked a few feet to peer up at the light pole. Sure enough, there was Marge's leopard-print garment, dangling from the camera.

CHAPTER 6

Despite her failure to discover whoever had been sitting behind her at the pool, Delphine had a little extra pep in her step as she strolled through the hotel grounds on her way back to her room. *Her* room! A place to herself! What a stroke of luck. She hadn't realized Marge and Kenji had gotten to the point in their relationship where they wanted to share a room, but apparently they were, and all the better for her. She'd have a ball on her own. A quiet, self-reflective, plenty-of-time-for-reading ball, if everything went smoothly. And why wouldn't it? This was her perfect vacation after all. She identified one possible drawback however: Her room was right next to Kenji and Marge's. She hoped the walls weren't too thin.

When they'd made their travel arrangements a few weeks earlier, the three friends had originally secured a single room for Kenji, and a room with two double beds for the women to share. The rooms faced the ocean but only came with tiny balconies. Delphine hadn't been pleased with that fact, but her room had been the last double-occupancy available in the entire resort. And now she had it to herself. It couldn't get much better. Her outlook brightened with each step she took.

She decided to take a shortcut and walk through the hotel's

main building. As she went through the automatic glass doors and into the lobby, Delphine heard someone call her name. She glanced around and caught sight of a woman at the check-in counter waving at her.

Delphine's eyebrows lifted in mild surprise at having been recognized, until her spy training kicked back in. They had cameras everywhere; of course they knew who she was. And as a particular friend of Mr. Conte's, the staff had probably been alerted to her visit before she'd arrived.

"Mrs. Lougheed?" said the woman who had called her over. Her name tag read *Leia*.

"Yes, that's right," said Delphine.

"We were instructed to give you this." Leia smiled and handed Delphine an off-white envelope with no writing on it.

"Thank you," said Delphine. She turned the envelope over a few times, wondering how she felt about it. Apprehensive? Excited? Who on earth could it be from?

She started to walk away but had a burst of inspiration and turned around to face the woman again. "I don't suppose you could check to see if there's another room I could switch to? Single occupancy."

Leia tapped at her keyboard. "Let's see what we can find."

Four minutes later, Delphine exited the lobby with a key to a third-floor, one-bedroom, ocean-facing suite with an extended balcony, and someone from the hotel staff to help move her bags. She dropped Kenji's laptop off at his room, where Marge was happily unpacking her things. Then Delphine and her helper gathered her suitcases from room 202 and took everything to the new suite, which was in a different but nearby building.

When they got to Delphine's suite, the resort employee, a young man who had made easy work of carrying her bags up and down the stairs, opened the door with his universal key card. He wheeled her suitcases into the bedroom, and she walked him to the door.

"Thank you so much for your help," she said, taking him by

the arm, which was much more muscular than she'd expected, but not in a bad way. She pretended to stumble and hung onto him a little harder. "I never could have managed all those heavy suitcases without your help." Before she let go of his shirt sleeve, she squeezed his bicep.

"Uh, no problem, ma'am," said the young man, who was quite handsome in a rugged, outdoorsy way. Ah, if only she were fifty years younger. She smiled, and he returned it along with a confused expression.

She held up two twenty-dollar bills. "Here's a little something for your trouble, cutie." Delphine put her hand into the pocket of his shorts and deposited the money there. Then she pinched his universal key card between her index and middle fingers, removed her hand from his pocket, and slid the card into the sleeve of her blazer.

"Thanks, ma'am," said the boy. As he went for the handle to close the door he gave her one more look of mild distaste, then left her alone. Oh well, it had to be done. One never knew when a universal key card might come in handy. Creeping out the young people was the price you paid sometimes for successful espionage.

Delphine took a quick tour of the suite and twirled a few times in the spacious living room. The whole place was nothing short of gorgeous, because Fausto had helped design it. From what she'd read, he had a hand in designing every part of the entire resort, from the bathroom tiles to the pathways made of lava rocks arranged in geometric patterns. His attention to detail was what made his films so rich and unforgettable too.

The mini-kitchen and gigantic bathroom featured sleek, minimalist fixtures. White walls throughout were contrasted by dark-wood trim, bright-colored printed textiles, and hand-carved wooden sculptures. The teak four-poster bed looked to be hand-carved as well, with a distinctly Hawaiian floral-print coverlet. Pillows on the couches matched the bed's decor. Stunning.

She took her mysterious envelope out to the balcony and made herself comfortable on one of the outdoor couches. The balcony railing was made of thin, sturdy metal, giving her an almost unobstructed view of Kaimoa Bay. She gazed at the sparkling water and sighed with contentment. A tall chain of mountains ran behind the resort and along the sides of the bay, making her feel like she was tucked into a comfy tropical safe haven. The breeze felt like a hug as it enveloped her in the perfect temperature. And the best part—it was so quiet! Just the sound of rustling vegetation and bird calls of all sorts. No cars, no trucks, no man-made noise. She could get used to this place.

Before they'd left Pasadena, Delphine had done some research on the island. Kaimoa Bay was located on the "windward" side of Mokumoa—the side that received all the rain and as the name implied, most of the wind. The extra rainfall caused the vegetation to be much greener and lusher than it was on the other side of the island—the leeward side. Here on the windward side, the locals grew cacao and even coffee. Bird and plant life thrived, and Delphine felt the vibrancy of the place in her very bones. She couldn't stop smiling.

Nonetheless, receiving an elegant envelope with no explanation was an intriguing development. She'd wanted peace and quiet. But maybe a little bit of intrigue or mystery might be fun? That didn't seem right. It ran contrary to her desire to retreat from the world for a few days.

What a disconcerting predicament.

Delphine placed the envelope on her lap and studied it for a moment. She picked it up again, carefully undid the back flap, and pulled out a single piece of thick, off-white card stock, which matched the envelope. Across the top, the name *FAUSTO CONTE* had been engraved in black ink using a heavy masculine font. Beneath it was a handwritten note, dashed off in somewhat legible cursive.

Delphine,
Wonderful that you have come to visit my resort. Why don't you stop by

the estate tonight at eight to say hello to Jasmina and me—we're having
a little party. Miko will bring you.
-FC

She smiled. Fausto and his wife happened to be on the island too—how nice. It would be fun to see them again. Of course she'd have to get hold of Miko, Griffin's new colleague and mentor, so he could take her to the estate. She'd ask her granddaughter about him at dinner.

But wait. She couldn't talk to Griffin about it at dinner. Marge would hear. And Delphine wasn't sure she had the energy to babysit Marge at a party at Fausto Conte's house, not after the Brock Celery scene. She wished she could wave a magic wand and bestow propriety on her friend. But life didn't work that way. If you considered someone your friend, you accepted all aspects of them. Unless you couldn't.

The jury might still be out when it came to Marge.

CHAPTER 7

The Club at Kaimoa Bay was an exclusive, members-only establishment, separated from the Resort at Kaimoa Bay by a mysterious wooden door set into an ivy-covered stone wall. Guests at the resort who wanted to add a short-term club membership to their holiday package could do so for a right hefty fee, and in turn received full access to everything the club offered—tennis courts, a salt-water pool, hot tub and sauna, plus an award-winning restaurant and bar. Marge knew all this because she'd read up on the place as soon as Delphine had invited her and Kenji along to visit Griffin.

It was six o'clock on the nose, and Marge and Kenji were the only ones who had made it on time for dinner. Marge considered it a major life priority to be on time for meals.

A server came by to bring them water, and Kenji selected a few appetizer platters for the table. When the server left to put in the order, Marge leaned over and gave him a kiss on the cheek.

"What is that for?" he asked.

"You know me so well," she said.

"Yes, I can tell you are extra hungry and about ten minutes away from getting cranky," said Kenji.

Marge laughed.

Here they were, enjoying the evening at an outdoor table of the club's swanky restaurant, with a view of the beautiful bay. Marge felt like she was a million miles away from everything, except for her awesome boyfriend Kenji, who was so close, she could reach out and poke him.

"Ouch!" he said when she reached out and poked him in the shoulder.

Kaimoa Bay was by far the fanciest place Marge had ever visited. And that was saying something, considering she'd been to some real swanky establishments in Florida with her pals the Blingsters. Those ladies knew swanky, but this was a whole other level of swank.

Delphine appeared at the edge of the patio and made her way over to take the last seat at the table with a view of the bay. "Sorry I'm a few minutes late," she said.

Marge scowled. "Why are you dressed so fancy?" Delphine wore navy-blue linen pants and a white silk flowy blouse. Usually Delphine's clothes were too boring for Marge's own taste, but this outfit looked pretty nice.

Delphine put a hand to the collar of her blouse. "This old thing?"

Before Marge could grill her friend any further, the appetizers arrived.

All the food had been beautifully plated, and everything else was fancy too, including the natural-colored linen napkins and the flower arrangement in the center of the table. Marge inspected the snacks and selected a baked pear topped with Gorgonzola and candied pecans. As she took her first bite, she closed her eyes and sighed with delight. Before she'd met Kenji, she'd had no idea such culinary wonders existed. Her preferences tended to lean toward Midwestern cookin'—she'd been born and raised in Oklahoma after all. But now her new boyfriend liked to teach her about the joys of cooking, and how to develop her taste buds. Or palate, as he liked to call it. He was so fancy. He'd been around the world and had a lot of knowledge to show for it. And he knew a crap-ton about food. Watch out Pioneer Woman, you've got competition!

When she opened her eyes again, Griffin was approaching the table in the company of a tall young man with wavy black hair and golden skin. He looked like a super-hot reincarnation of Thomas Magnum, the swoon-worthy fictional TV character who'd singlehandedly made the eighties worthwhile. Only this Magnum didn't have a mustache. But still. It seemed like Griffin's new job might be off to a good start.

"Hiya, Griffy!" said Marge. She stood to hug her granddaughter and Delphine did the same.

"Hi, grandmothers," said Griffin.

"Who's your friend?" Marge asked as Griffin and the handsome stranger sat down at the table. The man took the chair right next to Marge. He sure did smell nice—like salty air and manly shaving cream. The newcomers had their backs to the ocean, but Marge didn't feel bad since she would only be in paradise for a few days, while Griffin had the foreseeable future to enjoy the view. Of the hot guy and the ocean.

"Everyone, this is Miko Brown, he's my, um…" Griffin gave Miko a confused glance but instead of helping her out with an explanation, he smiled at her.

"He's showing me the ropes," she said. "And he tried to pick me up when I first got here."

"Oh, wonderful!" said Marge. "Did he take you where you wanted to go?"

Griffin shook her head. "No, I mean he hit on me."

Miko closed his eyes and rubbed the bridge of his nose.

Marge cooed with delight. "Even better! How did that work out? You two an item now?" She turned first to Griffin and then to Miko, waiting for an update.

"No," said Griffin in a definitive tone.

"It was a mistake," said Miko, sounding regretful.

"Thanks a lot," said Griffin.

"No, I mean…" Miko looked around the table at everyone staring at him. "I thought…"

Griffin said, "He thought I was a man."

Kenji tried to hide a laugh behind a short rib, unsuccessfully.

"I don't get it," said Marge.

Miko leaned forward in his chair. "They told me I was meeting someone named Griffin. That's a guy's name! I didn't know she was who I was supposed to be meeting. When I saw her, I thought she was a tourist."

"He hits on tourists," said Griffin, making it sound like she was translating. Maybe she was—man speak was hard to figure out sometimes.

"I think we understand dear," said Delphine.

"You do?" Miko asked.

Delphine said, "No, but it's fine."

"I thought I was supposed to be working with a man," Miko mumbled. He didn't seem to realize he was digging himself a deeper hole with every word he spoke. Marge felt a little sorry for men sometimes.

"Well, if you were gonna pick someone up, our Griffy would be the best someone," she said, trying to help.

"Anyway, it's all cleared up now," said Griffin.

"Absolutely," said Miko. "Now that I've gotten to know her, I'd never consider spending time with her."

Griffin's face turned red, and Marge realized if someone didn't step in soon, a nuclear war might start right at the table.

"I'm Marge, Griffy's G-ma." She pointed to Delphine. "And there's Delphine, Griffin's grandmother." She emphasized the word *grandmother*, trying to make Delphine sound stern and boring.

Delphine said hello, unperturbed by Marge's dig.

Marge took Kenji's hand, which unfortunately felt very greasy thanks to the rib he'd eaten. "And this is my boyfriend, Kenji."

Kenji gave Miko a slight bow of his head. Such a gentleman! Marge swooned.

"Aloha everyone," said Miko. "I just wanted to come by to introduce myself. I don't want to intrude on your dinner."

"Nonsense," said Marge. "Join us! The more the merrier."

Delphine said, "You're not intruding at all. Please, there's plenty of food."

"Thanks!" he said. Griffin smiled at him.

Marge got a buzzy feeling in her stomach. Had she witnessed a *moment* between the two youngsters? She sure hoped so. She'd always liked Magnum PI.

The young man inspected the platters of appetizers like a piranha who just got tossed into a pool of minnows. "If you're sure it's okay."

"Absolutely," said Kenji.

Miko loaded up a plate of snacks for himself. Everyone made small talk for a few minutes, and Miko gave them some background about the club and resort, which were both designed personally by the famous director, Fausto Conte. Marge didn't listen too closely; Magnum was distractingly cute.

They took a break from chatting to place their dinner orders, and before Marge knew it, the entrees had arrived. She tucked into her lobster ravioli with gusto.

"Aloha everyone!" A man dressed in a dark-blue shirt and white pants had stopped at the table.

"Hi, Davis," said Miko.

The man introduced himself as Davis Kama, the manager of both the resort and the club. Marge felt very much like an VIP and then felt like a mega-VIP when Davis announced they'd get to enjoy free food and drink for the duration of their stay, courtesy of Mr. Conte.

"Wowee!" said Marge. "Did we win some kind of lottery?"

"He's a friend of mine," Delphine said in a quiet voice.

Marge gasped. "How did I not know this?" But then she remembered why she didn't know. Because Delphine never talked about who she knew and what she'd done that had resulted in knowing said people.

"Please tell Mr. Conte thank you from all of us," said Kenji.

Davis said yes, he'd tell Fausto, and then told to let him know if they needed anything during their stay. He left, and the group went back to eating.

"Griffy worked for the FBI, did she tell you?" Marge said to Miko between bites.

"Really?" Miko asked.

Griffin nodded. "Forensic accounting mostly, but I also investigated structured—"

Delphine coughed loudly and shook her head.

"Accounting," said Griffin.

Marge was kind of happy to be spared a long, involved explanation of whatever it was Griffin used to do. It was in the past, why did it matter now, other than it sounded impressive to say her granddaughter used to work for the FBI.

"Maybe tell Mr. Conte, and he can put me to work on his investment team," suggested Griffin. "Instead of doing all these odd jobs."

"Instead of working with me, you mean," said Miko. He winked at Marge as he drank his water. Marge winked back.

"You just be sure our Griffy gets a fair shake, and also maybe take her on a date," said Marge.

Kenji looked at Miko and then Griffin. "Yes, a date sounds like a good idea."

"Oh my god," said Griffin, putting her hands over her eyes.

Miko kept his eyes on his plate.

A few minutes later, Delphine bored them with some kind of story about something involving rabbits. Or maybe palm trees. She wasn't sure. Darnit, Miko was so cute! But he had nothing on her Kenji. And neither did Brock Celery, truth be told. Although it sure had been fun to meet a movie star. And actually, Brock was pretty darn dreamy. She couldn't help but glance around the patio, in case he happened to stop by for dinner.

"What is there to do around here at night?" Kenji asked Miko.

Miko wiped his mouth with his napkin before speaking. "Hmm. Well, things stay pretty quiet at the resort, but over in town there might be some things to do. I can check to see if tonight is bingo night at the community center, if you'd like."

"Pish!" said Kenji. "What about dancing?"

"Yeah," said Marge. "What if we want to get our Hawaiian boogie on?" She wiggled in her chair. Griffin's face turned red, but Marge couldn't help it. When she felt the beat, she felt the beat.

Miko said, "I might have a place for you."

"Whaddya say, Big D? Want to come dancing?" Marge knew Delphine liked to go ballroom dancing, so she hoped Delphine would decline the invitation to boogie.

"I'd love to," said Delphine, and Marge's face fell. "But I've got other plans."

"You do?" asked Marge, Kenji, and Griffin.

Delphine looked stricken, like maybe she'd eaten something bad. "I mean, I'm not feeling well and plan to go back to my room for an early night. You two should go have fun though."

Marge scrutinized Delphine. They'd known each other a long time—Delphine's daughter and Marge's son had been married a while now. But in all those years, the two women hadn't spent much time together, and didn't know much about each other. But since they'd been roommates for a few months now, that had begun to change. Marge didn't believe Delphine's story about not feeling well and called her on it.

"Horse poop," Marge said. "You've got something going on. Spill it."

Delphine shook her head.

Now Marge knew something big was going on—Delphine wasn't even attempting a lie!

No one wanted dessert, so everyone at the table pooled together to figure out a tip for their nice server. Kenji got out his phone to order a ride to the disco bar.

"Miko, could I speak with you privately for a moment?" Delphine asked him.

"Of course," said Miko.

The two of them left the table and walked to the pool, where only a few people were still lounging in the water.

Marge watched them leave. They might be going, but they would not get away.

CHAPTER 8

"I'll be right back," said Marge. "I have to powder my nose."

"Does anyone even do that anymore?" asked Griffin.

"I believe it is an idiom," said Kenji.

Kenji and Griffin continued to yammer on about the origins of the phrase 'to powder one's nose' and Marge would've liked to learn more (not really), but she couldn't hear them anymore anyway because she had left the table on an important mission.

She headed first in the direction of the restaurant, under the guise of going inside the building to use the restroom. But at the last minute, she made a quick right turn and skirted the edge of the pool area. If she took the long way around and made it snappy, she might be able to hear Delphine and Miko's conversation.

She scurried in front of the bar, which was almost deserted, it being dinnertime. Next she jogged around the jacuzzi and along the path leading to the tennis courts. After picking up the pace to make it across the last stretch of ground to the other side of the pool, she installed herself behind the fattest palm tree she could find and stood for a moment to catch her breath. As luck would have it, she heard Delphine clear as a bell. Marge knew the conversation routine—she'd been the recipient of it many times.

First came a few lines of small talk, followed by Delphine trying to get Marge to do something, like unload the dishwasher, or take down the undies Marge had hung in the guest bathroom to dry. Nothing was ever straightforward with Delphine, and it drove Marge nuts. Taking the long way around was tiring and a waste of time. But tonight, it had worked in her favor.

Yes, it sounded like the small talk was finally coming to an end. Perfect timing.

"I've been invited to Fausto's party this evening," Delphine said to Miko. "His note said if I wanted to come, you would be able to take me."

"Oh sure, no problem," said Miko.

Marge stepped out from behind the tree. "I think Kenji and I will also attend that there party," she said.

"Marge." Delphine looked like she might explode.

Marge had never heard her friend sound so mad. Delphine hadn't raised her voice or said anything mean, but there was so much anger behind the single word.

"What?" said Marge.

"Where should I start," said Delphine, like she'd been forced to pick something out from the worst buffet line in the world. "This was intended to be a private conversation, hence my leaving the table. And … oh yes, right. You're not invited."

"I don't think Mr. Conte will mind," said Miko in a friendly tone. Now it seemed like Delphine might want to hit someone instead of explode. Miko was closer, so Marge felt fairly safe.

"Great!" said Marge.

Delphine scowled and crossed her arms. "Trust me, he'll end up minding."

"Now I take offense at that on behalf of me and Kenji," said Marge. "I mean, you can penalize me for eavesdropping I guess, but the rest of what you said was just rude."

"Um, I think I'll go back to the table," said Miko, picking up on the fact he'd landed in the middle of something unpleasant. Perceptive kid, like Magnum!

"We'll all go," said Marge. "So we can leave for the party together. Oh! Can Griffin come too?"

Honestly, Miko, you don't have to take anyone but me. Marge and Kenji were not invited." Delphine glared at Marge. "And Griffin is an employee of Mr. Conte, not his guest."

"Wow, D, you are harsh!" Marge shook her head. "She doesn't even want to go to a party with her own family."

Delphine's shoulders slumped and Marge knew she'd won.

CHAPTER 9

Delphine stood with Miko in the double doorway leading into a large living room, full of party guests. Griffin, Marge, and Kenji had already entered and gone to investigate a side table laden with glasses of wine and some snacks. Griffin seemed apprehensive, but Marge appeared to already be forming a plan for world domination.

Delphine still fumed about Marge inviting herself—and everyone else—along to the party. Decades of lying for a living, and for some reason she hadn't been able to keep her plans a secret from Marge. She'd hesitated to tell a lie at the dinner table about why she didn't want to go dancing. Her mind had gone blank, and that had been her fatal mistake. Marge was quick to identify and leverage weaknesses. She probably would've made a great agent.

"Are you sure it's okay they're here?" Delphine asked Miko. "Because I have no problem telling all of them to go wait in the car."

"Nah, it's all good," said Miko. "There's plenty of food and drink, plenty of room."

Delphine was worried less about the food, and more about potential impropriety. She hadn't seen Fausto in years; the last thing she wanted was to insult the man by bringing her own entourage to compete with his.

Miko must have noticed her concerned expression because he added, "Mr. Conte enjoys an audience. The bigger the better. Besides, it's good for Griffin to get used to this kind of thing. She might be helping out around the estate from time to time."

"How's she doing?" asked Delphine.

"Good! But she was a little grumpy when she first got here."

Delphine laughed. "Well, she's been through a lot recently."

Miko said, "I guess, but this is Hawaii. Everyone's super chill, you know?"

"I know," said Delphine. She hoped she'd feel more "super chill" soon.

Fausto Conte was easy to spot—he sat in a large armchair surrounded by guests, like a man holding court. The energy radiating from him felt larger than life, and the whole room seemed to buzz with activity.

Despite her own grumpiness earlier, Delphine resolved to enjoy the party. She took a deep breath and tried to calm herself. If Marge made a scene now, the woman would be on her own. Delphine would claim not to know her. Yes, perhaps it'd be best to stay split up from the rest of the group.

She felt a hand on the sleeve of her blazer.

"Delphine?" Fausto's wife, Jasmina, pulled her into a hug. "Oh, dear friend, it's been too long!"

"It has," said Delphine as the hug ended and she stepped back.

Jasmina's long dark hair flowed over her shoulders, drawing Delphine's eye to the plunging neckline of her black dress, which she filled in generously. Jasmina looked put-together, taken care of —but not in an I've-had-a-lot-of-work-done way.

"It's wonderful to see you again," said Delphine.

"Come, let's get you a drink." Jasmina led her away from the others.

Delphine turned back to Miko and waved goodbye. He gave her a thumbs-up.

"Delphine!" Fausto's voice boomed out, making the large room seem small. He stood from his chair and approached her with outstretched arms, leaving a crowd of bewildered guests behind. He wrapped her in his arms, and it was like being embraced by a lasagna. Warm, but not unpleasant, with a slight whiff of garlic.

"Hello Fausto," she said.

The years had been kind to her old friend. He was a few years older than she, but large sums of money seemed to afford those who possessed it better health than those who didn't. He wore a suit of tan, finely woven linen with a white linen shirt. His grey hair was a bit wispy on top, but otherwise intact. Yes, he still looked very fine, and she could see why she'd fallen for him so many years ago. That was back before his marriage, and hers, when they had been young and naive and idealistic, and the realities of life after college seemed very far away.

The three friends stood together and made small talk (how could they do otherwise, after going so long without seeing each other?). A server came by with a tray of wine glasses and Delphine was about to take one when Fausto caught her by the arm.

"I have something better," he said, pointing to a small parlor on the other side of the hallway from the living room.

Jasmina waved at someone behind her husband. "I've got to talk to Bunny about the art installation in LA," she said, and excused herself.

Fausto took Delphine into the parlor and riffled through several cabinets at the built-in bar. While he did so, she took the opportunity to survey the party. From her vantage point, she had a perfect view of everyone in the other room.

Marge, Kenji, and Griffin stood near a large fireplace, talking to Miko. Delphine kept her fingers crossed Marge wouldn't try any funny business.

One other figure caught her eye. A small-framed man stood among the group Jasmina was talking to. He wore a tuxedo with tails, which made him stand out, since everyone else had on more casual clothes. Strangely enough though, he didn't seem out of place in his formal attire. It suited him somehow. But the LA Dodgers bucket hat put the whole outfit over the top.

It was the man she'd seen at the pool in the afternoon. Their gazes met and he smiled.

Her stomach took a little dip, as if she'd just driven over a big pothole. It was strangely compelling. Exciting, but dangerous. But she couldn't explain it with any more precision than that.

"You've got a lot of people at this party for such a small island," said Delphine, still watching the stranger.

"Oh," said Fausto with a casual air, "you know how it goes. You've got friends, and then you've got *friends*, you know?" He had retrieved an empty glass from above the bar and now poured her a few fingers of eighteen-year-old Macallan.

The man in the tuxedo still watched her. "I do know."

"Anyway, I'm so glad you were able to make it," said Fausto, and Delphine swung her gaze back to the director. "Most people have jet lag their first day here. Plus, as I recall, parties aren't really your thing." He handed her the glass, a quarter full of a heavy amber liquid.

"As for the jet lag, I feel fine. You're right about the parties, although I've learned to tolerate them over the years." Oh, the parties she'd been to—mostly while on assignment. She and her team had attended many elegant affairs of all sizes, but when they weren't working, she preferred to stay home with a good book or maybe go dancing. She'd always had time to spend with Kenji though. "I imagine you still love parties," she said.

"I love parties and big dinners and spending time with my family," said Fausto. He took a drink of Scotch. "Except when I'm working. Then I need to sequester myself."

"That's understandable," said Delphine.

"Anyway, I want to hear all about what you've been up to all these years!"

Delphine laughed. "I don't think we have time for a full rundown. Besides, we have company." She pointed behind him and he spun around. There stood the man in the tuxedo.

"Ahem," said the man.

"Ah, yes!" said Fausto. "Delphine, let me introduce you to my friend Kapuni Jones."

Kapuni stepped up to join their small circle. He smiled at Delphine with his bright-white teeth, and she smiled back out of politeness. He reminded her of a shark—quiet but very dangerous. She glanced down and noticed he had on flip-flops.

"Aloha," he said in a quiet, calm voice. "Fausto has told me so much about you." He held out his hand.

"He has?" Delphine shook Kapuni's hand. It seemed to fit perfectly with hers. She looked at Fausto and said, "I wonder why he did that."

"Because you are two of the most interesting people I've ever met," said Fausto matter-of-factly.

Delphine snorted but regained her composure. "Fausto hasn't told me a thing about you, I'm sorry to say."

"We haven't been in touch for over fifteen years," Fausto reminded her.

"True," she said.

Fausto put a hand on her shoulder and peered into the other room. "Now if you both will excuse me, I've got to get back to my guests. We'll all catch up later, I promise."

"See you later!" Kapuni called after him as Fausto strode out of the room. Kapuni turned to Delphine. "We'll never see him again."

Delphine laughed and nodded. Fausto Conte promising anything having to do with "catching up" with someone "later" was about as binding as a wrist restraint made of al dente spaghetti.

CHAPTER 10

"Now let's see here." Kapuni retrieved a whiskey glass from above the bar, like Fausto had done. He opened a cabinet door, pulled out the bottle of Macallan, and poured himself a few fingers.

"You're probably wondering why I'm helping myself to Fausto's private stash," said Kapuni as he swirled the alcohol in his glass.

"Yes, I am," she said.

Kapuni studied his drink. "He would probably wonder too."

"What?"

"I'm just kidding, just kidding!" He wiggled his eyebrows at her. "I bought him that bottle. We are old pals. Stop looking so worried."

"I'll stop if you give me reason to," she said.

He stood opposite Delphine, and they watched each other carefully. "I will do my best."

Kapuni leaned one hand on the counter, relaxing his posture. He seemed perfectly at ease. He was fascinating, in a way, and almost seemed so devious as to give him an air of real innocence. But that didn't make any sense.

Did it?

Usually Delphine's intuition about people was impeccable, and she had little trouble identifying those who could be trusted and those who weren't worth the time and needed to be avoided. There had never been a need for a third category. But Kapuni Jones seemed to fall somewhere in the middle of the field, which felt very confusing. Delphine didn't like feeling confused.

She wanted to put one hand on the bar and lean back too, and also appear casual, although she didn't feel too relaxed. She stopped herself, lest the gesture come across as a retreat. And neither would she lean forward—it might convey interest. Instead, she chose to stand with a straight spine. Neutral.

"What shall we toast to?" he asked her, raising his glass.

"But we already drank," said Delphine.

"I know, but I forgot to toast."

"Good health?"

"Bo-ring," said Kapuni.

"It might sound boring but it's always worth toasting to," Delphine said. "Especially at our age."

"Pfffffft," said Kapuni. "Keeping track of birthdays is for losers."

Delphine couldn't hide a laugh. She felt the same way and wasn't sure why the words *especially at our age* had come out of her mouth in the first place. It had sounded so … old.

He raised his glass higher. "To the Dodgers!"

"To the Dodgers," said Delphine. She did like the Dodgers, but it seemed like eighteen-year-old Scotch deserved something more formal.

They took a few more sips from their glasses. The Scotch went down smoothly. She didn't particularly care for alcohol, preferring to keep her wits about her as much as possible. But she could still appreciate good quality when she tasted it.

She caught sight of Marge in the other room, hovering over the platters of snacks, while Kenji seemed to be having an animated conversation with Fausto. Griffin walked down the hall carrying a tray of empty glasses toward the kitchen. Goodness, had they put her to work?

"So you know Fausto from college," Kapuni said.

"How much did he tell you?" she asked. Fausto hardly knew anything about her anymore; she wondered what he'd said.

"He said the two of you are old friends, and you met at UCLA."

"Yes," she said. "How do you know him?"

Kapuni bobbed his head. "Same."

"You're lying," said Delphine. She would have remembered him.

"I am, yup," said Kapuni.

"Are you going to tell me how you know him?"

"Nope," said Kapuni.

Their gaze met, and Delphine held it, using the time to get more of a read on him. His sharp, steely-gray eyes assessed her right back. Once again, he reminded her of a shark. Never staying still, always moving. Was he assessing her for weaknesses, for a tender spot where sharp teeth might not meet so much resistance?

She kept her face blank. No one would get through her armor.

Or maybe she was projecting her own protectiveness onto him. Maybe she was the one who was filled with resistance. Her eyes lowered to her glass. When she brought them back up to his, he gave her a warm and genuine smile.

She took another drink of her Macallan. "I saw you at the pool this afternoon."

"I had a late lunch at the restaurant. Cool place, eh? I love that club."

"Mmm," said Delphine.

They stood together, not saying anything. She peered into the other room, where everyone looked like they were having fun. Delphine felt like she should make more conversation with her companion, as one did at parties, but she couldn't seem to do it. She felt tongue-tied, even though she was so very curious about him.

At Kapuni's suggestion, they rejoined the party in the living room. Fausto had begun to tell everyone about his upcoming film project, and the new movie from his grandson Marco "Mookie" Conte, who was already an award-winning documentary filmmaker at the tender age of eleven.

Marge and Kenji stood listening to the great director entertain his guests. Delphine excused herself from Kapuni's company and sidled up next to Marge.

"Where's Griffin?" she asked.

Marge looked around the room. "Oh! Well, I'm not sure."

Delphine spotted Miko standing in front of a bookshelf laden with expensive treasures and antique books. She slowly made her way over to him. "Where's Griffin?"

Miko smiled and tried not to laugh. His eyes darted to the door, and Delphine followed his gaze. Griffin walked in, looking haggard. She spotted them and headed their way, but halfway across the room she got stopped by a party guest who handed her their empty wine glass. Griffin took the glass, placed it on a nearby side table, and came to stand next to her grandmother.

"Everyone thinks I'm part of the catering staff," she said.

"I told you not to wear black and white," Miko said.

"I know," she snapped, "But I don't have a lot of clothes with me."

"Do we need to take you shopping, dear?" Delphine asked her.

"I'll be fine as soon as I get my first paycheck," said Griffin. "The first thing I'm going to do is buy some clothes that don't make me look like a waitress."

"I guess dressing for work Hawaii is a little different than dressing for the FBI," admitted Delphine.

Miko turn sideways so they weren't all lined up against the wall. "Hey, I saw you met my uncle," he said to Delphine.

"Excuse me?" Delphine asked.

Kapuni Jones walked up to join them. "Hello, Nephew," he said to Miko.

CHAPTER 11

Delphine quirked an eyebrow. "This gentleman is your uncle?" she asked Miko.

Kapuni Jones grinned and stepped up next to Miko. "He is my nephew." He put his arm around the taller, younger man. "The whole family is very proud of this kid. Even though he didn't go into the family business."

"What is the family business?" she asked.

Kapuni gasped and put a hand over his mouth. "That's kind of a personal question."

Delphine tried to cover up a yawn but did a terrible job at it. Jet lag was really catching up to her. Maybe she should leave soon. The party guests had thinned out quite a bit. Marge and Jasmina sat on the sofa, deeply engaged in a discussion about jumpsuits. Kenji was nodding off next to Marge. A few minutes earlier, Griffin had finally given up collecting dishes and had gone to the kitchen, refusing to come out.

"Are you read to leave?" Miko asked Delphine.

She nodded. "Yes, it's been a long day."

Miko's phone pinged, and he pulled it out from his pocket. "It turns out Griffin and I need to stay here and make sure the caterers get packed up."

"Need to escort them off the premises?" Delphine asked.

Miko smiled. "Something like that, yes. But I'm afraid I won't be able to give you a ride back to the resort. Uncle, would you mind—"

"I would love to," blurted Kapuni.

"Oh no, we can't ask you to do that," said Delphine, unsure she wanted to get in a car with this person.

Kapuni pulled his phone from his tuxedo breast pocket and sent a text. "It's no problem. Momi will be here in a few seconds."

"Seconds?" asked Delphine.

He nodded. "She's very fast."

Delphine was too tired to ask more questions. She and Kapuni gathered up Marge and Kenji, and all four of them said thank you and good night to Fausto, Jasmina, and Miko. They walked out the front door and onto a short path leading to the circular drive. As soon as Kapuni's flip-flop-clad foot hit the gravel road, a sleek black Mercedes came barreling up, almost sliding to a stop in front of them.

"Oooh, sweet ride!" said Marge. "It's just like the one I used to have!"

The words sent a chill down Delphine's spine, as she knew how Marge had managed to afford such an expensive car. An AMG E 53 was a lot of car for a lot of money. Perhaps this particular model of Mercedes was the go-to choice for those who came by their fortunes in questionable ways?

A very pretty and very young Hawaiian woman emerged from the driver's side wearing a black pantsuit with a white button-up shirt. Long black hair flowed out from under an LA Dodgers cap. She opened the back door on the passenger side.

"Thank you, Momi," said Kapuni as he got in.

Delphine's eyebrows rose. She wondered what else Momi did for Kapuni other than drive his expensive car.

Delphine went next, followed by Marge. Kenji got ushered into the front passenger seat.

Momi slid in behind the wheel and pulled her Dodgers cap

farther down onto her head, as if preparing for a rough ride. Before Delphine could contemplate what the implications of that action might be for herself and her fellow passengers, the car took off so fast the backs of their heads slammed against the headrests and were stuck there, thanks to the incredible rate of acceleration. The faint sound of gravel spraying out from under performance tires was the only sound they heard other than the leisurely purr off the engine.

Momi navigated the Mercedes off the private gravel drive, through several residential streets, and onto a main road without ever coming to a stop. She tore along the road like a woman on a mission, weaving through traffic and riding bumpers.

On a particularly sharp left turn, Delphine knocked into Marge, who said into her ear, "It's like we're in a video game!"

Delphine nodded but said nothing. She gripped the seatbelt strap across her waist with one hand to prevent herself from knocking into Kapuni on her left, or Marge on her right. The middle position in the back seat of a video game car was not the ideal place to be.

Marge leaned forward and asked Momi, "How do you like the suspension in this thing?"

But it was Kapuni who answered. "It's a little stiff out on the open road but we manage."

Marge nodded. "That's what I thought too. Drove like a truck on the freeway sometimes."

The price one pays for luxury, thought Delphine, who was also a big of a Mercedes fan, but very happy with her lowly E-class.

When the car came to an abrupt stop ten minutes later in front of the Resort at Kaimoa Bay, everyone's head jerked forward and at least two seatbelts locked up.

Kapuni jumped out, ran to the other side of the vehicle, and opened the door for Marge and Delphine.

"Thanks for the ride, Kappy it was fun!" said Marge as Kenji got out and put his arm around her.

"It's Kapuni," said Delphine.

"That's what I said," said Marge.

"You're welcome," said Kapuni. He gave Delphine a puzzled look. "Kappy?"

"She likes to give people nicknames," she explained.

"What is her nickname for you?"

Delphine laughed. "Like I would tell you."

"No matter," said Kapuni. "I'll consider it a challenge to find out. See you guys soon, aloha!" He jumped back into the car and it sped off, accompanied by the sounds of screeching tires. Delphine wondered where he might be going in such a rush.

CHAPTER 12

Delphine, Kenji, and Marge walked into the resort lobby. Delphine tried to think of a way to break off from the group and sneak off to her suite. She was tired, and in no mood to have to explain her room change to her friends; they'd probably give her a hard time about abandoning them for a better location. Well, nothing was stopping Marge and Kenji from going in together and paying for a bigger suite too, so too bad for them. But still, Delphine didn't want to deal with any of it tonight. All she wanted was a bubble bath and a nice big bed.

Marge and Kenji slowed their pace, and Delphine stopped to wait for them. "Is something wrong?" she asked.

"No," said Marge, clearly hedging.

Delphine sighed. Was she really so scary that everyone was afraid to tell her things? She usually tried to come across as kind and interested, but tonight her patience was wearing thin.

"We are going out dancing," said Kenji. He checked his phone. "Our ride will be here in three minutes."

"We're gonna go check out the club Miko told us about in downtown Kaimoa Bay. Do you want to go?" asked Marge. Her voice sounded inviting enough, but her eyes said *please stay home*.

Delphine tried to thwart another yawn. "Thank you for

inviting me, but I think I'll turn in for the evening. You two have a great time but be careful."

"Okie dokie," said Kenji. "Come on, Super Babe, let's boogie!"

Marge waved goodbye and they went back outside to wait for their car.

Delphine had to laugh. Surely Kenji and Marge felt as jet lagged as she did, yet they wanted to dance the night away. Maybe Marge had been right; maybe Delphine was now in her dotage.

Delphine made her way through the dimly lit lobby and out the back door. She took the path leading to her building. When she got to a second path, which led to the building she'd moved out of, she paused. She felt tired, but also wired, like she'd missed the window to go to sleep and now would have to wait for the next one to open. She turned down the second path and headed for room 204—Kenji's room.

For some reason, she couldn't get Kapuni Jones out of her thoughts. Who was this person? Besides being charming, intelligent, polite, and apparently wealthy, he also seemed to be aloof, evasive, and eccentric. She wanted some facts.

As she climbed the stairs to the second floor, Delphine pulled her universal keycard from her purse and went the short distance down the exposed walkway to Kenji and Marge's room. In one swift motion she let herself in and locked the door behind her.

The lamp on the side table next to the couch shone a dim light through the small space. Everything seemed quite tidy, except for the bed, which was covered with a huge selection of Marge's jumpsuits. Delphine didn't want to take the time to look, but she bet Marge had already hung swimsuits and undergarments all over the bathroom, from every available hook or bar—just like she did in Delphine's guest bathroom back home in Pasadena. Delphine once again thanked her lucky stars she'd snagged a room to herself.

Now, where would Kenji stow his laptop? A quick perusal revealed his messenger bag lying on the small office desk in one corner of the room. Delphine opened it up, but it was empty except for his travel documents, a tin of breath mints, and a bruised apple. There was no sign of the computer anywhere around the desk, so she expanded her search to the couch and side tables, the dresser drawers, the mini bar, and even the mini fridge (cold storage for electronics wasn't the greatest idea, but they'd all had to do it at some point in their espionage days).

No laptop.

Delphine grimaced at the thought of getting into her friends' personal lives any more than she already had, but now she was a little worried about the laptop, which seemed to be missing. She searched the bedroom area and under the pillows on the king-size bed, under the bed, and in the closet.

No laptop.

Next came the bathroom. Yes, Marge had hung bits of clothing everywhere, but Delphine found no computer.

In her rational mind, she knew it was quite unlikely for Kenji to lose his laptop. Surely it was in the room somewhere, she just couldn't find it. But spies didn't always work in the rational realm. Good spies relied on instinct as well as logic. And her instincts were giving her some not-very-good news.

Delphine pulled out her phone and texted Kenji, telling him they might have a problem, and to please return to his room as soon as he could. Chances were slim he'd notice a message while at a dance club, but she had to try. As luck would have it, he responded right away, and said he and Marge would be back in twenty minutes. Delphine unlocked the security latch on the door so they could get in and went out to the tiny balcony to admire the view.

The bay was protected from the high winds that hit other parts of their side of the island, so the waves were very small. If fact, the tiny ripples on the water could hardly be called waves. The moon, which peeked out from behind racing clouds every so often, lit up the water's surface and made it sparkle. She could've sat there all night … if she wasn't so worried about a stupid computer.

It seemed like only seconds passed until she heard Kenji and Marge unlock the door and come inside. She reentered the room to greet them.

Marge shimmied her way over to the couch and fell into the cushions as Kenji relocked the door. Neither of them seemed surprised to find Delphine waiting for them inside their room.

"Did you have fun?" Delphine asked Marge.

"Sure did!" said Marge. "But I tell you what, I was downright pooped after fifteen minutes. Dancing still sounds fun, but maybe my boogeying days are over."

Delphine studied Kenji. His hair was damp, and he'd sweat through his aloha shirt. He went over to the mini bar area, picked up his stainless-steel water bottle, and took a deep swig. "Maybe we will try ballroom dancing with you, Delphine."

"You're both welcome to join the Foxy Trotters for open house night," said Delphine.

"But I don't think you made us come back so you could ask how we are feeling," he said.

Delphine frowned and sat down next to Marge on the couch, who was now fanning herself with the room service menu. "No, I didn't. Kenji, where's your laptop?"

"Right here." He walked to the tiny desk, and for a moment Delphine wondered if she'd remembered to check the desk drawer. Kenji picked up his messenger bag and it almost flew out of his hands because he hadn't expected it to be so light. "Well it *was* right here."

CHAPTER 13

Kenji felt his heart start to race, but he took a deep breath and tried not to jump to conclusions. Marge had taken his laptop at the pool earlier in the day, saying she had wanted to keep it safe for him. Perhaps she had done it again this evening, before they'd left for dinner.

"Super Babe, did you put my laptop in a super-safe place?" He opened the desk drawer and searched all around the desk and minibar but found nothing. He came to the couch and sat down on the other side of his girlfriend.

"Nuh-uh," said Marge. Her eyes were closed, and it looked like she was about to melt into the sofa cushions. "Honestly, I forgot all about that thing. You should too."

He wished at this point he could forget all about it; he wished it with all his might. He glanced at Delphine for help, but her face remained expressionless. "Let me check a few more places," he said.

Five minutes later, he'd searched every place he could possibly think of within the confines of the hotel room. No computer.

"So it's really missing?" Marge tried to sit upright but seemed to be too tired to prop herself up. Kenji offered her a hand and pulled her to sit straight.

"I'm afraid so," said Delphine.

Marge stood up on wobbly legs and walked to the balcony. "Well, isn't that a kick in the pants! You wouldn't think this fancy resort is the kind of place where stuff goes missing right out of your room."

"I don't think it is," said Delphine. She gave Kenji a pointed glance.

"We should talk to the manager guy. What was his name? Davis something-or-other. They need to know their resort is a den of thieves!" said Marge.

Kenji scratched his chin, which now had a day of stubble on it. It gave him a tiny thrill to think back to the week before, when Marge had said she loved his stubble because it felt scratchy on her neck. Scratchy in a good way, she'd said. Oh, he couldn't wait for later, after Delphine left…

Except now he seemed to have a very big problem. "Was there any sign of forced entry when you got here?" he asked Delphine.

"No," said Delphine. "But as you know, that doesn't mean anything."

"It doesn't?" asked Marge, coming back to the couch from the sliding glass door.

"I didn't have to break in to get in here, so it's very possible someone else could've gotten in the same way," said Delphine.

"Oh," said Marge, sounding more worried now.

Kenji laughed. "I wonder how many universal key cards the front desk is missing this week. Besides the one you have."

His moment of humor turned into dread faster than he could say *stolen laptop* as the realization of what had happened set in. Why had he ever agreed to do some work this week? He was filled with regret. But Charles Bing, the director of the Western States Division of the Falls, had personally reached out to him three days earlier and asked for a special favor. Kenji had explained he was going on vacation, but Director Bing said it would be okay to take the laptop with him. And now he'd lost it. He was going to get in soooooo much trouble.

"How would someone know you had a laptop to steal in the first place?" asked Marge.

It was a good point, Kenji thought.

"Well, your boyfriend did practically wave it in everybody's face at the pool this afternoon," said Delphine.

Kenji's index finger shot out in an accusatory jab. "You used it too!"

Delphine lowered her eyes to the floor and swung them back to Kenji with a concerned expression.

"What?" asked Kenji. Then he got it. "Oh, you are wondering if someone has broken into your room as well."

"Don't be ridiculous," she said.

But he was right. It probably hadn't happened, but he knew she was wondering if it had.

"Ha!" said Marge. "I guess you shoulda brought a fingerprinting kit with you, like the CSI people have on TV."

"Yes, ha-ha," said Kenji in a humorless voice. He admonished himself for not bringing his travel fingerprint-dusting kit. He'd thought about it but decided against it at the last minute. Which had been a mistake, it turned out.

"There's one other thing," said Delphine. She picked up a business card that had been lying on the coffee table, next to the TV remote and a few local magazines. "Have either of you seen this before?"

Kenji took the card from her. It wasn't a business card, but rather a calling card. On one side, a telephone number had been handwritten in an incredibly tidy and precise block print. The other side featured a letterpress-printed graphic of a boat. The design was a simple line drawing, but it was easy to tell the boat was supposed to be a fishing trawler, complete with a winch and pulley system from which dangled a little net.

"Huh," he said.

"What is it?" Marge snatched it out of his hand and inspected both sides. "I don't know what this is."

"Me neither," said Kenji. It was becoming apparent someone

besides Delphine had invaded his and Marge's privacy at some point during the evening. Honestly, he didn't mind when Delphine did it. Heck, he broke into her house all the time too. It was kind of nice knowing your best friend could get to you—especially if things ever went bad in a hurry. And he had nothing to hide from her. But from other people? He wanted to hide just about everything from everyone else.

"Does the drawing look familiar?" asked Delphine. "I can't seem to place it."

It didn't ring any bells for Kenji either, but Delphine was the visual specialist. He knew numbers and facts; she thought more in pictures. "I don't recognize it," he said.

"So someone came in here, took your computer, and left you a calling card," said Delphine.

"That's plain weird," said Marge, yawning.

"Not really," said Kenji. "All things considered." Considering their past, he meant.

"All things like what?" asked Marge.

Kenji glanced at Delphine, whose eyebrows rose, waiting for him to answer. He had been debating how much to tell Marge about his past as an international spy. He wanted to tell her everything, he really did. But he wasn't convinced it would be in anyone's best interest. Knowing could put her at risk, and the more people who knew about his and Delphine's past, the bigger chance of a slip-up.

"Considering what we used to do for a living," he finally said.

Marge put her hands on her hips. "I still don't know what that is exactly. And not knowing is starting to irk me."

"Maybe we could discuss it on another day," suggested Delphine. "Or at least after we've all gotten a little more sleep."

"No," said Marge, sounding like a petulant child.

"No what?" asked Delphine.

"No more keeping me out of the loop. You guys tell me everything or else," said Marge.

Kenji yawned. "Marge, sweetheart, it is late." He'd managed

to avoid telling her very much up till now, and didn't think the middle of the night on their first day of their first vacation together would be a good time to start.

Marge paced around the room. "Well what are we gonna do with this?" She held up the calling card.

"I don't know," said Kenji, and it was the truth.

"They want you to have their number," said Delphine, thinking aloud. "I suppose because they don't have yours."

Kenji crossed his arms. "They probably do by now." If someone had managed to log onto the laptop, they'd have a lot more than his phone number.

"Let's call it," said Marge.

"Not yet," said Delphine. "We need to think this through."

Marge stopped in her tracks in front of the TV. "For Pete's sake. It's probably just some dumb kid who wants to make a couple of bucks selling your laptop back to you. He left you his number, so you call it." She paced again. "You two are not very smart sometimes."

"I agree with Delphine on this one," said Kenji. It wasn't wise to act without thinking things through, especially when you were tired. And *especially* especially if the logical course of action seemed a little too logical. He let out a long exhale.

"Is there anyone else you need to call?" Delphine asked Kenji in a low voice.

"I can still hear you," said Marge.

"I know dear," said Delphine.

"Yes, I will have to make a call," Kenji said in a matching low voice. "But not right now. Maybe I will try to find it first, before..." Before he'd have to call his boss and admit a very bad thing had happened on vacation. Kenji fell into his thoughts, wondering what, if anything, should be done in the middle of the night about a missing computer while suffering from wicked jet lag.

"Okay, enough," said Marge. She marched over to Kenji and pulled his cell phone out of the pocket of his aloha shirt. He didn't give the action much thought, figuring she wanted to check what time it was. He wondered too, come to think of it.

Marge sat down heavily on the couch with the card and the phone and tapped at the screen. "There," she said a few seconds later.

"What?" Kenji started to get a bad feeling in the pit of his stomach.

Marge huffed. "I'm sick and tired of you two. Always planning and plotting—without me, I might add—and never taking action. It's like you're both too intellectual!"

"What did you just do?" Kenji asked. The pit in his stomach now felt like a giant rock quarry of doom.

"I sent a text to the number on the card."

Delphine closed her eyes and rubbed her temples. "Oh boy," she whispered.

Kenji started coughing and felt like he couldn't stop. He sprung from the couch and grabbed the phone from Marge.

"What did she do?" asked Delphine in a raspy voice.

"I'm right here you know," said Marge. "You can ask me directly."

He read the text out loud. "I want my laptop, you scumbag."

Delphine got up from the couch, stretched, and said, "I think it's time for me to leave."

CHAPTER 14

Delphine said goodnight to Kenji and Marge and left them sitting on opposite ends of the couch. She shivered as she walked down the steps of the building. It seemed their first night together had gotten off to a great start.

Respectable guests were all asleep in their rooms at this hour. Perhaps a few adventurous souls were still out having fun somewhere, but in any case, Delphine saw no one. The Norwegian people popped back into her mind. She wondered where they were right then. She stopped and looked around, as if merely thinking about them might cause them to materialize in front of her. But no one appeared.

She was dead tired, but being lost in her thoughts, she accidentally took the wrong path. Instead of going directly back to her suite, she found herself walking past one of the resort's three pool areas.

Delphine tried not to think about the fact that basically, her dream for a peaceful, quiet vacation had been blown right out of the water on her very first day. She should have known better than to think such a thing were possible. She could always refuse to help Kenji and let him figure out his own problems. She could get some peace if he went off to play detective without her. But even though they were retired, and even though they weren't romantically involved, it still felt like they were a team. And she couldn't let him down.

She took a deep breath of the warm night air and slowed her pace. Why not enjoy being outside under the dark, wide-open sky. A light covering of clouds rushed by overhead, and the breeze whispered through the palm and plumeria trees. It all felt like romance.

Delphine believed the past should stay in the past, but it still popped its nostalgic head up at unexpected times. One never traveled through grief in a straight line. She had lost her Charles long ago, but some days she missed him as if it had been yesterday.

The stone path now led her past the swimming area's entrance gate. A gentle cough coming from the direction of the pool caught her off guard and she jumped. A closer inspection revealed a lone figure reclined on one of the lounge chairs by the water. The man's legs were crossed at the ankles, and he'd pulled a bucket hat low over his eyes to shield his face from the nonexistent sun. A Dodgers bucket hat, to be exact. Kapuni Jones had changed out of his tuxedo jacket and back into shorts and a T-shirt.

Maybe she should've been surprised to see him lying there, but she wasn't.

Delphine walked up to the pool gate. "A little late for swimming, no?"

"This is the best time to catch some rays," said Kapuni Jones, uncrossing his ankles and recrossing them again. He made no other attempt to move.

"Agreed," said Delphine, although she had no idea what he'd meant. She pulled the universal key card from her blazer and opened the gate. When she got closer, she noticed a small ice chest sitting on the ground by his chair. Beside the cooler rested a backpack and a pair of flip-flops.

She sat down in the lounger next to his and wondered if the little cooler might be filled with something sinister, like illicit drugs, or someone's thumb. Or wouldn't it be ironic if Kenji's laptop were stowed away in the backpack? She really needed some sleep.

Without sitting up, Kapuni reached down and popped the lid off the cooler, and her muscles tensed in anticipation. She couldn't bring herself to look inside.

"Want one?" He pulled out a can of Pabst Blue Ribbon and held it up.

On any other day, she'd decline. But tonight was already a lost cause, and a PBR sounded perfect. "Thank you," she said, and took the can, feeling brave enough to peer down into the cooler.

It only held five more beer cans. Four, after Kapuni took one out for himself.

Delphine popped the top, which made a satisfying *pffft* sound, and he did the same, again with a friendly *pffft*.

She sipped some beer, he slurped his. Neither of them offered any conversation. She became frustrated by the silence, but also more intrigued, despite her better judgment. Her instincts told her to walk away. But they also told her to stay put. It was infuriating. Also enthralling.

"Did you enjoy the party?" he asked.

Delphine rotated the beer can in her hands; one revolution clockwise, one counterclockwise. "It was good to see Fausto and Jasmina again, yes."

Kapuni nodded. "They are good people."

"Did you meet them here on the island?" she asked, trying again to learn more about him.

"Yes, but no," he said.

Delphine pursed her lips and considered leaving; she was in no mood for non-answers.

"I mean, we had mutual business partners in LA, so we knew about each other for a long time," Kapuni said. He must've realized he was about to lose his audience. "But we met in person here on the island." He waved his hand dismissively.

He sat up in the pool chair so suddenly it startled Delphine. "I wanna ask you out on a date," he said.

Delphine's eyebrows shot up, then reversed course and floated down to land in a furrow.

"Why?" It came out of her mouth before she could censure herself.

"Because you are enchanting." he said, and finished off the rest of his beer.

Delphine took a large drink from her can as she considered his words. Enthralling, enchanting ... apparently they were close to being on the same page.

"Well," she said, not knowing what to follow it with.

"We'll have a nice time. Good dinner maybe. Watch the sun set on the other side of the island." He removed another PBR from the cooler and offered it to her, but she shook her head.

She wondered what exactly his idea of a good time might be. Here was someone who drank expensive whiskey with Fausto Conte but also loved PBR. Someone who drove a luxury car but also eschewed shoes. Someone who seemed harmless yet reminded her of a shark.

Kapuni pushed his Dodgers hat farther back on his head and watched her, waiting for an answer.

Conflicting feelings began to tap dance across her chest. Kapuni felt a little dangerous. But he was also kind of cute. Did she want to start something up with a stranger? Did she want to start something up, period? Was she ready for romance? Would it be okay to simply have a little fun on vacation?

"What about Momi?" she said. Asking about his beautiful driver was a diversionary tactic, although she was genuinely curious.

"What about her?" Kapuni sounded confused.

"Who is she to you? Are you and she..."

"Uncle and niece? Yes."

"Oh," said Delphine.

"She just graduated from college and needed a job. I told her mother I'd look after her. We are trying to dissuade her from becoming a Formula 1 driver." Kapuni swirled the beer in his can.

Delphine smiled. "That might not be possible."

Kapuni laughed. "I know, but I'm trying."

They sat there a moment more while Delphine struggled with what to do.

What would it hurt?

What wouldn't it hurt?

"So, you'll let me take you out?" Kapuni asked. Delphine noticed he had very bushy eyebrows.

"No thank you," she said.

His expression remained the same—almost. She registered a hint of disappointment around his eyes and felt bad about it.

"You sure?" he asked.

Delphine wanted to say no, she wasn't sure at all. She wanted to explain that while she saw at least a dozen bright-red flags when she so much as glanced in his general direction, her heart also told her saying no might lead to an even bigger regret than saying yes. But she couldn't say any of those things; she could barely admit them to herself.

"I'm sure," she said. "But thank you."

Kapuni nodded and slurped some more beer. "You'll tell me if you change your mind," he said, making it into more of a statement than a question.

"Yes," she said, and stood up. "Thank you for the beer, but I'd best go back to my suite and get some sleep."

"Of course. Aloha," Kapuni said, holding up his can of beer as a goodbye gesture.

"Aloha," said Delphine. She deposited her beer can in a trash receptacle at the gate and left the pool area. She didn't turn around to look at him one last time, although she wanted to.

When she got back to the peace and quiet of her luxury suite, she inspected everything and determined no one had been there while she was gone (she didn't think it had ever been much of a possibility, but she'd also learned you'd better check anyway). She took a quick bath and climbed into bed with a paperback but nodded off without reading a single page. She turned out the light and went to sleep asking herself why she'd said no to a date with Kapuni Jones.

CHAPTER 15

Marge floated in and out of sleep, listening to the sound of the ocean breeze in the palm trees outside the open hotel room window. Or maybe the sound was more like waves. Yes—gentle waves lapping against a dock. Rhythmic, sawing waves cutting through petrified wood. She opened one eye and remembered she was lying in bed with Kenji, who happened to be sawing logs like a professional lumberjack. She reached over and nudged his arm, and he rolled onto his side and stopped snoring.

The sky was still dark. The bed felt like feathers and her pillow was the most comfortable one she'd ever used. She wondered if she could stuff it into her suitcase when they left. The pillows at Delphine's house were all either too poofy or too flat. Disappointing, really.

The events of the previous night trickled back into her consciousness. Kenji never did hear anything back from whoever she'd texted on his phone. She couldn't understand why he and Delphine hadn't approved of her decision to do it. Take action! That was how to get things done. In any case, she and Kenji hadn't gone to bed mad, which was good, considering it was the first time they'd spent the night together.

Marge drifted off to sleep again and landed in a strange dream involving birds. Thousands of birds, sitting on a breakfast buffet and pooping in the scrambled eggs. Next thing she knew, she was being prodded awake by her boyfriend.

"Marge," said Kenji in a soft voice.

He had a very sultry voice when he wanted to, like right now. But she could do without the poking. It wasn't the good kind of poking.

He jabbed his finger into her upper arm again. "Super Babe."

With a jump, she awoke fully and sat up. "Over easy!" she yelled. "What the what?"

Kenji pulled his hand away. "It's me, Kenji," he said. "From last night?"

"Oh goodness gracious," said Marge. "I guess I forgot where I was. Must be jet lag." She yawned. "Now what's so important you had to wake me up in the middle of the night?"

"It's almost six in the morning," said Kenji.

"Oh. Hey! Did you hear anything about your laptop?" she asked, hoping for some good news.

Kenji frowned. "Nothing yet. But come check this out."

He helped her out of bed, and they went out onto the tiny balcony.

"You're real cute in those jammie shorts," she said, pointing to his legs. He had great legs.

"Thank you," he said, trying to stand up taller.

"Did you bring me out here to show off your gams?"

"What? No." He pointed to the sky, which had started to lighten.

Overhead few hundreds of snow-white birds, squawking as they glided by with their legs pointing straight out behind them. They seemed to be coming from a copse of trees down by the beach, heading inland.

"Holy moly!" said Marge. "That's a lot of birds."

"Cattle egrets," he explained.

She looked at him with wonder in her eyes. "You know everything," she said in a dreamy voice.

He flashed her a satisfied smile and pulled her close. They watched the lanky birds fly overhead. Their first morning waking up together, and it was perfect.

"Last night was nice," said Marge.

"Yes. Very nice," said Kenji. He sighed. "I am sorry I fell asleep as soon as we got into bed though."

"Oh, K-Man, it's okay. It happens to all of us at one point or another. Especially at our age."

"I guess, but I don't want you to take it personally."

Kenji was truly the sweetest man ever. The truth was, she probably would have taken his nodding off personally, if she hadn't been so dadgum tired herself. She'd fallen asleep right after he had.

"One question though," said Marge.

"Oh yes, tonight, for sure," said Kenji.

Marge waved a hand at him. "No, not that."

"Okay, what?"

"Delphine has the room next to us, right? Room 202?"

"Um, yes," said Kenji.

"Then who is that on her balcony?" Marge tilted her head a tiny bit to the right instead of using her finger to point.

Kenji looked where she'd indicated. "Ohhhh."

A young woman stood on Delphine's balcony, naked as all get-out. She too gazed up to admire the cattle egrets. Her long blond hair fell away from her shoulders as she tilted her head to the sky.

"My stars," said Kenji.

"I'll say," said Marge. The woman did have a nice set of stars. "Either our Delphine has some new hobbies we don't know about, or something is super wrong."

"It is probably nothing."

The woman's silhouette showed off a lot of curves. "It looks like a whole lot of something from here," said Marge. She went back inside, picked up her cell phone from the nightstand, and called Delphine's phone.

"What are you doing?" asked Kenji, poking his head into the room.

Marge held up her palm and he stopped talking.

"What do you want? It's not even six o'clock," said a sleepy Delphine.

"Good morning to you too," said Marge.

"Unh," said Delphine.

"Who is out on your balcony?" Marge whispered into her phone as she crept back out to join Kenji, who was still engaged in some not-very-subtle spying.

Delphine yawned. "What? Let me check."

Marge waited to see Delphine walk out onto the balcony. Delphine did not appear, but a second naked woman emerged to join the first one. The two embraced.

"My stars," said Kenji and Marge.

The sound of their voices caught the attention of the two women, who turned in their direction. They smiled and waved and went back into the room.

"Oh," said Delphine. "That's just maintenance. They came by to get a lizard off my deck chair."

"Room 202?" Marge asked tentatively.

"Yes," said Delphine.

"They sent two ladies?" Marge tried to confirm.

"It was a big lizard."

"What an interesting hotel this is," said Marge. "I had no idea we were in a nudist resort. This changes everything."

"What on earth are you talking about?" said Delphine, sounding more awake now.

"Wait," said Kenji. "I did not agree to stay at a nudist resort. Nudity with strangers is not my bag."

"It didn't seem to bother you too much two minutes ago," said Marge in an irritated tone.

"What is going on?" asked Delphine. "Put Kenji on the phone."

"She wants to talk to you." Marge held the phone out to him.

"Oh no," said Kenji. He raised both hands over his head to avoid taking the device. "It is too early in the morning. I need caffeine before I can mediate for the two of you."

"Never mind," Marge said to Delphine. "Sorry to wake you. We'll let you get back to your entertaining."

Kenji tried to convince Marge there had to be some sort of logical explanation for the women next door besides Delphine having made some significant lifestyle changes in her later years, but Marge remained unconvinced. The only way he could get her to change the subject was by offering to order room service.

Marge ate with gusto to her heart's content. Everything seemed to taste better when someone else paid for it.

Kenji seemed a little down, probably because of his laptop.

"Are you going to let a computer ruin your whole vacation?" she asked him as they finished up their breakfast.

"No," he said, but he didn't sound very convincing.

"I told you not to bring that thing," she said, feeling like the world would be a much better place if everyone took her advice.

"Well I did, and now I need to get it back," he said.

Marge got up from the tiny two-person dining table and sat on his lap to give him a hug. "Don't worry, K-Man. This will be a super fun day, and I'm sure by the end of it, you'll have your dumb computer back." She gave him a smooch.

After another cup of coffee each, the couple left the room for their first paddleboarding lesson, compliments of Delphine.

CHAPTER 16

Kenji checked his phone one last time and put it back in his messenger bag. No texts. Not from Delphine, and not from the mysterious number on the calling card. It was nerve-wracking, but what could he do? He could go to hotel security, of course, or the police. But it was still too early in the game. He and Delphine always tried to resolve an issue on their own first. They considered asking for help to be an action of last resort.

He looked out at Marge, standing by the water. Their paddleboard lesson started in two minutes. She waved and flashed him her big, beautiful smile, and he almost melted on the spot.

"C'mon, K-Man, I saved you a board," she called. She pointed to the two paddleboards by her feet.

"Okay!" he said.

His phone pinged from inside his bag. Probably just Delphine checking in, but he needed to make sure. His breath caught when he saw the screen. He'd received a text from the mystery number —a response to Marge's demand from the night before. He scanned it quickly.

> 555-555-5555: We are watching you and your girlfriend. We know what you both used to do. If you want your computer back, you will present us with USD $2,000,000 Tuesday afternoon or we tell your superior and leak information to your enemies.

Kenji glanced up and down the beach. Were they watching him right now? He felt vulnerable, and protective of Marge. Wait … the ransomers knew what kind of job Marge used to have? How did they know what she used to do? He didn't even know what Marge used to do. At one point she'd worked in a drugstore, he was pretty sure. Then it hit him. They probably meant Delphine.

He needed to show the message Delphine as soon as possible, so they could analyze it together. He was about to text her, when Marge called out again.

"Yoo-hoo!" she yelled, sounding a little more impatient this time.

Kenji put his phone away. He felt terrible. There was his beautiful girlfriend standing on the beach, waiting for him to join her. But this mess with the laptop couldn't be ignored. Too much was at stake. Like so many times before, he had to make a choice between his personal life and his professional one. He regretted with all his heart ever agreeing to part-time consulting. But he'd have to wallow in regret later. Right now, he had a harder decision to make. Although it wasn't a decision at all. Work would have to win out again.

"I can't believe they don't let us go in the water on the first day," said Marge as he came up to stand with her.

"They don't?" Kenji tried to sound interested and not like his mind was a million miles away.

"Nope. Apparently we have to learn about 'safety,'" said Marge, using scare quotes. "So dumb."

"Safety is never dumb, Super Babe," said Kenji.

She put her hands on her hips and squinted at him. "I bet you were a hall monitor in grade school."

"How did you know?"

"Lucky guess," said Marge.

The class started, and the instructor, a very nice-looking lady, introduced herself to the class of six students. She had them go down the line and give their names and say something about themselves.

"I'm Marge from Oklahoma!" said Marge, adding an enthusiastic wave for emphasis. "This is my first time in Hawaii and my first time paddleboarding. When do we go in the water?"

The instructor politely explained to Marge—apparently for at least the second time—they would be allowed in the water the following day; this first lesson consisted of an intro to the equipment followed by a practice session on how to fall off the board properly.

"Like I need help falling off things," mumbled Marge.

Next came Kenji's turn to introduce himself. "My name is Kenji. This is my thirty-seventh time in Hawaii. I am looking forward to learning how to paddleboard."

"Have you ever done it before?" the instructor asked.

"No," he said, "but I went through Navy SEAL training once, so I imagine this is similar."

He glanced at Marge, who had an expression of awe on her face. "My boyfriend is a SEAL," she said on a sigh.

Once everyone had their turn, the instructor gave each person a life vest and they all practiced putting them on and taking them off. Five times. Marge cursed under her breath but complied, as did Kenji, but without the cursing.

Kenji checked his watch. He hated to use subterfuge on Marge, but it was the only way. He needed to talk to Delphine as soon as possible.

He put on his life vest for the sixth time and carefully placed his feet on the paddleboard, which was firmly planted in the soft, fine sand. Here goes nothing, he thought.

He inhaled deeply, let his knees wobble, and took a nosedive off the board. "Aaaaiii!" He face-planted with the agility of an experienced practitioner, although to the common eye, it came across as a real-live accident. After rolling twice (one roll wasn't usually enough to add sufficient drama and confusion), he came to a stop on his back and clutched at his right wrist. A grimace completed the performance.

"Kenji! Snuggle bear!" Marge ran to his side, followed by the instructor and the four other students.

"I fell off the board," moaned Kenji. He rolled to his side and Marge helped him sit up.

Marge had tears in her eyes and Kenji's heart broke a little bit. "Are you dying?" she asked.

"Maybe," said Kenji.

"Students, this is why we don't go out on the water on our boards until we've had our first safety quiz," said the instructor. "Imagine if this had happened in the bay and you hadn't put your life vest on properly."

She helped Kenji to his feet and once he was stable, he cradled his right elbow.

"I thought you hurt your wrist," said Marge.

"I hurt my wrist, yes," said Kenji, realizing his mistake. "But the pain is radiating up the major tendons in my forearm. I think I need to go see the nurse."

"This place has a nurse's office?" Marge asked the instructor.

The woman nodded. "Sort of. They can check him out in Davis's office. Can you walk okay?" she asked him.

He wanted to explain he'd hurt his wrist, not become a feeble oldster in the course of ten minutes. But he could see how it might appear like he had. "I can walk just fine. I will go back to the club and talk to Davis. Miss Paddleboard, I release you of all liability, do not worry. I am sure this is a superficial injury."

Kenji walked back to the chairs under the palm trees to get his messenger bag. Marge came up behind him. "Want me to go with you?"

He shook his head. "You stay here and have fun. I think you will like standing on the board and pretending to paddle through the sand."

Marge have him a loud smack on his cheek. "Okay. I'll come find you when we're done. See ya!" She bounded off to rejoin the group.

There was probably some sort of special karmic gift for people like him—for those who lied to their girlfriends. He left the beach with his head hanging low.

He walked to the club's restaurant, where Davis Kama's office was located. As soon as Kenji was out of sight of Marge and the paddleboards, he took off at a run. When he got to the pool, he stopped and texted Delphine.

He sent the text and heard the ping of an incoming message a few feet away.

CHAPTER 17

Delphine had just finished breakfast with Griffin at the club's restaurant and decided to sit by the pool. Griffin had run off to help Miko with some sort of symposium starting in the resort's conference room later in the afternoon, so Delphine had a few moments alone. She put her tote bag on an empty chaise longue and her phone pinged. She dug it out of her bag and saw the text from Kenji right as he walked up to her. He looked tired, like he hadn't gotten much sleep. Although she didn't want to know what had kept him awake on his first night together with his girlfriend.

On closer inspection, his expression turned out to be one of worry, not happy exhaustion.

"Did you hear something?" she asked.

"Yes," said Kenji.

"Where's Marge?"

Kenji pointed to the beach. "She is learning how to paddleboard."

"How'd you manage to get out of the class?"

"I had to fake an injury. Which is difficult, while you are learning how to not fall off a board," he said.

Delphine was confused. "I'd think it would be easy—just pretend to lose your balance and splash! You fall off."

"Yes, but we were paddling on the sand," said Kenji.

"Oh," said Delphine. "I guess that would be a bit awkward."

He nodded.

"So do you have something to show me? I'd hate to think you fake-injured yourself for nothing."

Kenji tapped his phone screen a few times and handed the device to her. She read the text.

"Interesting," she said.

"I thought so too," said Kenji.

Delphine sat down on the lounge chair. "I'm so sorry you have to deal with this."

"Really?" he asked.

"Of course. Why would you think otherwise?"

Kenji sat on the neighboring chair. "I assumed you will continue to admonish me until I find the stupid computer."

Delphine smiled. "I thought about it, but that approach doesn't seem very practical. A better approach would be to try to find your stupid computer, and then we can all get on with our vacation." And she could get some peace and quiet for more than five minutes at a time.

"I like your plan," he said. "But this message poses more questions than answers."

She agreed. "We know what they want, and we know what they'll do if they don't get it. But yes, there are a lot of questions here." She read the message again.

"I wonder if they are bluffing about telling my superior. That is a very vague threat."

Delphine tapped her finger on her bottom lip. "That part is vague, but other parts aren't." She had Kenji open his phone again so she could reread the note. "They're specifying USD. If they were American, they probably wouldn't have thought it necessary to specify the currency."

"Unless they are crypto bros," said Kenji. "But these people use complete sentences and spell out whole words."

"It also reads like maybe they think I'm your girlfriend. Or they happen to know what Marge used to do when she lived in Oklahoma. Which seems unlikely."

"And I don't think English is their first language," said Kenji.

Delphine didn't think so either.

She handed Kenji's phone back to him and they sat facing each other, not saying anything. Her mind raced with possibilities, and she felt a sort of invigorated excitement. The thrill of the chase perhaps. Or like the anticipation one felt when sitting down to start a jigsaw puzzle. Only this situation was probably more dangerous than a puzzle.

This wasn't a game; this was real life. Kenji stood to lose his laptop, and both of them might stand to lose much more. Excitement with an edge of heightened stakes.

She watched Kenji's face as he thought. She knew him well enough to know he felt the same way.

"The part about leaking information is concerning," said Kenji.

"Agreed. And that's why we can't ignore this whole thing."

He nodded. "Do you think they know who my superior is?"

"I really have no idea," she said.

"They could be here right now," said Kenji.

Delphine's eyes roamed around the pool area. "Hmm. Maybe."

"But maybe Marge was right and it's just some hotel employee stealing things. Maybe the person is nowhere near here."

"People," said Delphine.

"What?"

"The text uses the pronoun 'we.' There is more than one."

"A theft ring?" he asked.

Delphine sighed. "I don't know."

"But you do know something," said Kenji, pointing at her. "I can tell."

"Something about this feels familiar, in a removed sort of

way," she admitted. She shivered and suddenly felt chilly, even though they'd gotten another perfect day in their tropical paradise.

"That doesn't make sense," said Kenji.

"I know. Maybe it will at some point."

Kenji clutched his bag to his chest as if getting ready to leave. "I can get the money of course, no problem."

"Let's see if we can nip this thing in the bud before you pay up. But maybe call Frances and have her start liquidating some funds for you. Meanwhile, I want to enjoy a little pool time while I mull it over."

"This is Sunday," said Kenji. "I can maybe sell some crypto today but I can't do much about moving the money until tomorrow."

"Frances will take care of it, I'm sure," said Delphine.

"I guess. Well, I will go back to the beach now." Kenji stood to leave.

"Oh, wait one minute." Delphine picked up her bag and searched through it until she found what she wanted. She handed it to Kenji.

"What is this?" he asked.

"Marge's swimsuit cover-up. She left it here yesterday." Delphine had asked Miko to have someone pull it down from the security camera earlier in the morning.

"Okay, thank you," he said, and stuffed it into his bag.

A restaurant server came by and asked if they needed anything. Delphine ordered a Pellegrino with lime.

"Do you have any Ace bandages?" Kenji asked him.

CHAPTER 18

Twenty minutes later, Kenji had found an Ace bandage in Davis Kama's office and wrapped up his wrist with the precision of a medical practitioner. He'd then made his way back to Marge and the paddleboard lesson.

Delphine had suggested they check in later by text, but for now she sat alone on the beach in front of the resort. She'd wanted a quieter spot than the pool at the club, so she'd gathered her things and walked down the beach, away from the paddleboarders and the activity of the club. She found a quiet spot under a palm tree and set up camp.

She'd picked up her book several times but kept reading the same paragraph over and over until she finally put it down for good and allowed herself to doze off. It had been a late night, after all.

Delphine woke up with a start and opened one eye to survey her surroundings. All was still in order. She had the stretch of beach to herself—how lucky! Her book rested on her stomach and a sweaty glass of Pellegrino sat on a small table to her left. She had no idea what time it was, and she didn't mind not knowing.

Her position in the chair, the breeze, the mixture of sun and clouds in the sky, the faint sound of small waves lapping on the sand… All of it came together to produce a profound sense of contentment she hadn't felt in a very long time. Yet she was wise enough to know it was temporary, as all feelings were. Sooner rather than later she'd have to get back to the laptop problem. But for now, all was well.

Delphine had arranged for Kenji and Marge to go on a midday guided hike to some nearby tide pools, so they were still out of her hair, and she had a little more time to herself. The hike coincided with low tide for optimal viewing of the marine life living in the rock crevices and also included a snack on the beach. The food cost extra but Delphine knew how much Marge loved her snacks.

She would've liked to go on the hike herself—when she was little, her mother used to take her down the Southern California coast to visit the tide pools at Corona Del Mar. They'd pack a lunch and spend the day in the little cove. They watched the tide go out, and walked along the rocks when the water got low enough. In high school, she'd even thought of becoming a marine biologist, but her parents pushed her to study law. And today, having some alone time outweighed reliving childhood memories with Marge and Kenji. She could reminisce when she got back to LA.

Delphine sighed and closed her eyes again, overcome with an unpleasant sensation. She felt a little restless.

It was probably due to worry about the laptop and the implied threats in the text Kenji had received. But if she were being honest, what she really felt was excitement.

Could trying to relax be causing her consternation? Could she be … bored?

Preposterous. She wanted rest. Needed it.

She swung one leg over the edge of the chair and stuck her big toe into the sand. The fine particulate was still cool in the shade, and she contemplated sitting up and walking down to the water to let the gentle waves of the bay lap at her feet. In fact, she'd been thinking about getting out of her lounge chair for at least an hour, but hadn't yet mustered enough enthusiasm to actually do it; she was too comfortable.

Comfortable and relaxed.

But also restless.

Lazy but antsy was sometimes a dangerous combination—at least it had been in the past.

Delphine swung her leg back onto the chair and crossed her ankles. Her mind wandered again to the previous night's events and to Kapuni Jones, the mysterious stranger. She knew nothing about him, yet she'd been fascinated.

Captivated but uninformed.

Also a dangerous combination.

She closed her eyes and scowled at her silliness. Thinking about intriguing men was certainly silly. This was her precious alone time. She'd wanted nothing but alone time. But now maybe she wanted something else.

"We could always go for a walk," said a voice to her right.

She wasn't sure what surprised her more—the fact someone seemed to have read her thoughts, or the idea that someone had snuck up on her without her noticing. So much for remaining vigilant.

She let her head loll in the direction of her visitor. There was Kapuni Jones, fully reclined in the chair next to hers. He wore his LA Dodgers bucket hat pulled low over his eyes. Same faded black T-shirt and chino shorts as the first time she'd seen him. No shoes at all today. His hands were interlaced behind his head, and he looked like he might be sleeping, but sharks never slept.

"Okay," she said.

Kapuni hopped up out of the lounge chair with the spryness of a much younger man and offered her his hand. She let it hang unaccepted as she floated into a sitting position (she still had great core strength, thanks to yoga), and to her feet. Kapuni's hand fell to his side, and she smiled politely to indicate she'd meant no ill will. He smiled back, but his intention was unreadable.

Delphine put on her sun hat, which she'd placed under her

bag so it wouldn't blow away and adjusted her sunglasses. After smoothing out her dress, she put her book in the bag and slung the tote over shoulder. They strolled down the beach, in the opposite direction of the resort and Fausto's estate, and toward what appeared to be a neighborhood of large expensive homes.

They walked for several moments, Delphine right along the water's edge, Kapuni taking the inland side. They passed a few rows of lounge chairs belonging to the hotel, and Delphine got the feeling someone had eyes on her. She turned her head in Kapuni's direction and smiled at him but used the opportunity to scan the chairs over his shoulder from behind her sunglasses. She saw no one.

"You look weird," said Kapuni.

"Heartburn," said Delphine, rubbing her sternum.

"You should eat less processed food," he said.

"Is that so." The joke was on him, thought Delphine—she didn't eat processed foods.

They continued down the beach in silence.

Fortunately, long stretches of silence didn't unnerve Delphine. After her long espionage career, it took a lot more than a few minutes of walking along a beautiful beach with a complete stranger to put her on edge.

However, after several more minutes of silent walking, curiosity began to get the better of her. He'd invited her on a walk, yet he had nothing to say? How had he found her, anyway? Delphine smiled at the odds of meeting someone as adept as herself at finding people.

"What's so funny?" Kapuni asked.

When he looked at her, he had to squint, since the sun was behind her. She made a point of shuffling her feet to splash some water around. It made her feel coy.

"I was just thinking," she said.

"Oh yeah?"

"Yes."

Kapuni adjusted his hat. "Huh."

They walked on.

"You're retired now, eh?" he asked. "From your fishy business."

"I am retired, yes," said Delphine, not missing a beat. "But I was never in the fish business." Well, except for the whole Norway thing. Her chest tightened the tiniest bit. She'd tried so hard to forget about those trips to Norway, but now there seemed to be reminders everywhere. She shook her head in frustration. That was one of the problems with being a retired spy—you saw trouble everywhere you went.

"Of course no real fish. But fishy business. Like, questionable."

She raised an eyebrow at this. "You seem to know a lot about me."

Kapuni raised a shoulder. "Fausto was excited about your visit. He told me many things. You and he used to be great friends, he said."

"It was a long time ago," said Delphine. "He doesn't know much about me anymore."

"It's… It was kind of my job to know a lot about people," he said.

"You're retired now?"

Kapuni nodded. "No, not really."

"What line of work are-were you in?"

"Fish business," he said.

"Questionable?"

"Fishy fish."

Delphine felt a headache coming on.

Kapuni barked out a laugh. "Just kidding! I used to be a weather forecaster."

"Really?"

"No."

They walked another five minutes; this time the silence felt companionable, not competitive or concerning. They eventually came to a low stone wall running alongside a path which led inland from the beach.

"You wanna go eat tacos?" Kapuni asked, pointing down the trail. "Right down at the end of this street is the best place for 'ono fish tacos."

One side of Delphine's mouth slid up in deliberation.

"Not a date," he said, lifting both hands in a gesture of innocence. "Only tacos."

It seemed a reasonable invitation. And by Delphine's reckoning, it was close enough to lunch time. Tacos sounded good. "I could eat."

Kapuni nodded and they turned onto the sandy path.

CHAPTER 19

They walked up to the little restaurant, which resembled a shack more than a dining establishment. The outside of the place had been painted bright yellow. Against the wall next to the door leaned a plank of scrap wood which had the words *'ONO SEAFOOD* hand-painted on it in red paint. Delphine winced when they entered; the interior seemed a little questionable, with its torn vinyl booth seats and peeling wall paint in an unflattering shade of pale yellow. But *'ono* meant delicious, so she would give the place a try.

Kapuni ordered for them both—tacos filled with fresh-caught grilled mahi-mahi covered in some sort of savory, mayo-based sauce, and homemade mango salsa. The lunch specials included a side of potato mac and a drink.

They went back outside, and she chose a shaded picnic table in the small patio area adjacent to the building as he got their drinks at the soda fountain. He returned with two Cokes, heavy on the ice. Just the way she liked it, when she allowed herself her annual soft drink. They slurped in companionable silence.

When their restaurant pager went off, Kapuni went inside and came back with two compostable to-go containers filled with food. They began eating, and neither of them said a word because everything tasted so good.

"This is very 'ono," said Delphine after she'd eaten one of her tacos.

"See, I told you!" said Kapuni. He pointed his spork at her and smiled proudly.

"What is potato mac?" Delphine poked at the mound of white food on her plate. They'd used an ice-cream scoop to serve it.

"Potato salad and macaroni salad all together," he said. "Island specialty. Try!"

She speared some on her spork and nibbled at it. Her eyes closed in comfort-food bliss. She'd found a new favorite thing.

"Good, eh?" he asked.

She opened her eyes. "Mm-hmm. Do you like it?"

"Oh yes, I love it! This place has the best potato mac too. But I rarely eat it."

"Because it's processed food?"

"Yup. Gotta keep healthy, you know?"

Delphine did know. "Well, I'll make an exception since I'm on vacation."

"Good idea," he said, and scooped up some potato mac from his own container.

After finishing her second taco, Delphine was stuffed; she took one more bite of potato mac and put down her spork, satisfied and happy after finishing such a good meal. As she sat looking around the patio, she couldn't get over how wonderful the breeze felt on the bare skin of her arms and legs.

"Since you know so much about me, I did a little checking up on you," she said.

Kapuni put a hand to his chest. "Me?"

"It's kind of part of my job to know a lot about people too."

"Oh, I'm honored! Okay, so what did you find out?" he asked, sounding eager to hear.

Delphine frowned. "Not much, actually."

Kapuni laughed, but Delphine wasn't amused.

Early that morning, as soon as she'd woken up, she'd called her friend Judy Espinosa, who worked as an administrative assistant for the Falls. Judy used to report directly to their old boss, Richard Dere, who was a class-A idiot and now spent his days in prison for cheese smuggling. Judy still did favors for Delphine from time to time; they'd become friends over the last few months, ever since they'd taken Richard down.

Since Delphine couldn't use Kenji's "stupid laptop" to snoop, she'd asked Judy to perform a check in the Falls' databases on one Kapuni Jones. Judy found a speeding ticket from 1984, but nothing since then. The man was a ghost. Delphine couldn't ask Judy to dig too deep; neither of them wanted to get in trouble.

"All I know is you liked to drive fast in the eighties," she said.

"Ah, the eighties," said Kapuni, gazing skyward. "I remember that decade fondly. What a time of gluttony and unbridled greed."

Delphine tried not to laugh. She couldn't tell if he was serious or not, and that was part of the fun.

"Do you live in the neighborhood we passed by on the way here?" she asked, pointing out to the beach.

"Those big giant rich-people houses? Nah. Those are for, how should I say it … for people who do not originate from the islands." He sipped from his straw and made a loud slurping noise, having already finished the small amount of Coke in his cup full of ice. He took the lid off and peered inside the cup, then put it all aside.

"Coke is a processed food," she pointed out.

He flashed his shark grin. "I am an enigma."

"You'd like to think so," said Delphine.

"You just said you know nothing about me!" said Kapuni.

"Maybe not," said Delphine. "But you're not very hard to figure out."

His face drooped with disappointment. The male ego was so fragile. Like an underdeveloped eggshell.

"You must live fairly close though, since you showed up at the resort without shoes," she said, redirecting.

"Nope," he said, but didn't elaborate.

"Is there a Mrs. Jones?"

Kapuni eyed her with amusement. "Somewhere out there, probably. It is a common last name."

"While I find your personality borderline charming, you seem to be bordering on the edge of obtuseness."

He leaned forward with his elbows on the table. "You know, I am sorry about that," he said. "I'm not used to dealing with someone as sharp as you."

"Now you sound ingratiating," she said.

Kapuni sighed. "And you are almost annoying. I love it."

They grinned at each other.

Kapuni stood and picked up the empty to-go containers. "Ready to walk back to the hotel?"

She nodded and got up, and they left the little restaurant.

The sand was hotter now that it was past midday, so they walked in the shallow water along the shoreline.

"Your nephew seems nice," said Delphine.

"Which one?" asked Kapuni.

"Miko. The one who works for Fausto?"

"Oh yeah. Him. Yes, good kid, I like him. Shame he didn't go into the family business though."

"You mentioned that the other night. What is your family business?" She tried again to extract information.

"He went to college to play basketball," said Kapuni, ignoring her question. "Not good enough to go pro after he hurt his knee. So he went to work for the government. Can you believe it?"

"What's wrong with working for the government?" asked Delphine.

Kapuni lightly touched her shoulder. "Nothing at all, I didn't mean to offend you or your family. It's just... Well there isn't much money in it, is there."

Delphine couldn't tell if the slight elevation in her heart rate was due to his hand on her shoulder, or because he seemed to know what her family did for a living. But no way could that be the case. However, she couldn't think of any other explanation.

"Look, you need to tell me how you know so much about me and my family," she said sternly.

"I do?"

"Yes."

"Okay, here is the truth." He moved a little closer to her, near enough that they could talk in a whisper. "I know nothing about you or your family, except for what Fausto told me. But you seem guarded, particularly about your career history. What makes you think I know anything?"

Delphine pondered the question. She couldn't call him on anything specific without admitting he'd been right. But by getting upset she'd given herself away anyway, to a certain degree.

Maybe he really did know nothing. But every so often he looked at her or spoke in a tone that made it seem like he had something on her. What it might be, she had no idea.

Kapuni put both hands to his chest. "I am a very nice guy. Ask anyone and they'll tell you."

"That's what worries me," said Delphine.

CHAPTER 20

Delphine, Kenji, and Marge met up at an outdoor table at the restaurant later in the afternoon for snacks. And also so they could figure out what they wanted to do about Kenji's missing laptop.

Delphine had let the whole thing turn over in her mind a few times. She often gave herself time to let facts combine with intuition. Her process was perhaps tinted by memory, but always rooted in reality.

Davis Kama brought them a selection of appetizers and small platters, and the three friends filled their plates with snacks. Delphine was still full from her fish taco lunch, but couldn't resist the delicious-looking spread. She picked out a few grilled shrimp and pieces of fresh sushi.

"How were the tide pools?" she asked.

"Very interesting," said Kenji.

Marge made a grumbly, complaining sort of noise.

"I found it informative and beautiful, but Marge did not have as much fun," he explained.

"I got attacked by a gang of hermit crabs," said Marge.

"A cast," said Delphine. Marge stared at her. "A group of hermit crabs is called a cast, not a gang."

"Oh lord," said Marge. "Count on you to know the nerdy version."

"I also knew a group of hermit crabs is called a cast," said Kenji. He kept his eyes on the table, as if embarrassed by his confession.

"Yeah, but when you say stuff like that it's fascinating and sexy." Marge pointed to Delphine. "When she does it, she's being a smarty pants. And anyway, all I know is a whole bunch of them came after me and attacked my foot. Look!" She slid around in her chair to show Delphine her left foot. The tips of all her toes were pink, like they had been nibbled.

"It just means they like you," said Delphine.

Kenji leaned over and kissed Marge on the cheek. "It is because you are so sweet."

Marge giggled.

"I see your arm is better," said Delphine, pointing at Kenji's wrist.

"How did you know he hurt himself earlier?" asked Marge.

"Oh, um, he texted me," said Delphine.

"Huh," said Marge.

Kenji's eyes went wide. Delphine couldn't tell if it was because he'd gotten caught in a lie, or because Marge was upset he'd been in contact with someone besides herself.

"Yes, uh, I seem to have made a miraculous recovery," he said, rolling his wrist around.

"Praise be!" said Marge.

Indeed, thought Delphine.

"So no other communication with that phone number" Delphine asked Kenji.

"I would have told you," he said.

"Give me your phone K-Man, I'll make 'em respond," said Marge, holding out her hand to Kenji.

"I think you've done more than enough," said Delphine. "We couldn't possibly impose on you again."

"It's no trouble," said Marge, not seeming to get the sarcasm.

Griffin appeared at the table with her colleague Miko. "Got room for one more?" she asked.

"Of course!" said Marge. "There's room for two more. We're always happy to see you and Magnum! I mean, Miko." She pointed to the two empty chairs at the table.

Miko flashed an embarrassed smile and said, "I can't stay, but Griffin's got the rest of the day off."

"Aw darn," said Marge. "I mean, yay for Griffin, boo for you."

Griffin sat down at the table.

"Aloha, see you guys later," said Miko. He gave everyone a little wave and left.

As he walked away, Marge and Griffin watched him go. His long legs took easy strides, and Delphine recognized his athletic prowess in his movements.

Marge sighed and Delphine cleared her throat.

"What?" said Marge.

"He's too young for you," said Delphine.

"I know," said Marge in a wistful tone. "He sure is a tall drink of iced tea though."

Griffin nodded. "I guess."

"He is a sexy Hawaiian basketball-playing god," said Kenji, without looking up from his phone screen. Delphine figured he was checking for messages.

Marge pointed in the direction Miko had gone. "You should totally hit that," she said to Griffin.

"G-ma!" said Griffin, who sounded mortified.

Delphine laughed. "Well, I'd phrase it differently, but I have to agree with your other grandmother. It wouldn't hurt you to have a little fun. You're in a tropical paradise, and you just got divorced. It's time for you to relax and enjoy."

Kenji lifted his head. "I agree." He put his phone on the table next to his plate and went back to snacking.

"Yup, he kinda gives ol' Hottie McHotterson a run for his money," said Marge.

"Who is Mr. McHotterson?" asked Kenji.

"He's the police detective in Florida who arrested me," explained Marge. "Delphine, what was his real name? I forgot."

"Roland Magnusson."

"Oh, yes, Rolly!" said Kenji with a smile. "I did not know his alias was Hottie McHotterson. Peculiar undercover name."

Marge put her glass down so forcefully some Pellegrino sloshed out. "You know Detective Hottie?"

Kenji nodded. "Yes, we are pals."

"Well butter my biscuit! What a coincidence," said Marge. "How did I not know this about you?"

"When you think about it," said Delphine, "how much can we really know about another person?" She surprised herself with her words. She must have been thinking about Kapuni Jones again.

"What's that supposed to mean?" snapped Marge.

"Again, not helping, Delphine," mumbled Kenji.

"If it makes you feel any better, G-ma, I didn't know Kenji was acquainted with McHotterson—I mean Roland," said Griffin. She looked at Delphine. "Have you heard from him?"

"Not in a while, no," said Delphine. Griffin didn't know Roland had come to Los Angeles to help her get out of her cheese-smuggling predicament, and it would be better if her granddaughter stayed in the dark about that incident, otherwise Delphine would have to explain the cheese mess and she'd rather not think about it anymore.

"Oh," said Griffin, sounding disappointed.

"You could call him, you know," said Delphine.

Griffin seemed to perk up a bit. "I suppose I could."

"Yeah, but why would you want to call some grouchy old cop when you have Magnum PI right here?" asked Marge.

"I hate to interrupt this fascinating conversation about Griffin's romantic life, but could we focus on our little problem for a moment?" asked Kenji.

"You mean your big problem," said Delphine. Kenji groaned.

"What problem?" asked Griffin, selecting a few snacks to put on her plate.

Delphine swung her gaze to Kenji, who shrugged. Meaning, he didn't mind if she explained to Griffin what had happened. He was also probably curious as to why she'd want to. Delphine didn't necessarily want to tell everyone about their business, but Griffin was family. And perhaps it was time Griffin knew a little bit about Delphine's past. Perhaps it might even be time to bring her into the family business. And it was a family business—both of Delphine's children had worked or currently were employed by the Falls. Even her beloved Charles had worked there. Griffin was certainly smart enough to take on the challenge, if she chose to at some point.

Kenji would understand her logic for explaining everything, so she told the story. Or most of it, anyway.

"Someone has stolen Kenji's laptop." She put up her hand to stop Griffin from interrupting, and went on to explain how Kenji had brought his work laptop on vacation, and it had disappeared from his room. She described the highlights of the ransom texts and emphasized their desire not to involve the police.

"What kind of work do you do, Kenji?" Griffin asked when she'd been cleared to speak again.

"Well…" said Kenji.

Marge leaned forward in her chair. "I'd like to hear this too."

"Delphine and I used to do some … high-level advising." Kenji sighed heavily. "We worked together for many years. We retired a while ago, but I still pick up consulting work from time to time."

As Delphine predicted he would, Kenji broke into his best *Godfather* impersonation and complained about getting pulled back in just when you thought you were out. Griffin looked perplexed.

"Haven't you ever seen *The Godfather*?" Delphine asked her.

"Um, no," she said.

"Oh, you have to watch that movie," said Kenji. "American classic. Absolute must."

"I can't believe you've never seen it," said Marge.

"Okay, fine, I'll watch it," said Griffin. "But until then, I have no idea what you're talking about."

Kenji shook his head in a young-people-today-make-me-sad way.

Griffin tapped the table with her fingertips as she thought. "Something tells me your consulting was of an interesting and sensitive nature."

Kenji laughed. "You have no idea."

"That's just it," said Marge. "I really have no idea. So why don't you tell us?"

"Let's leave the specifics for another day," suggested Delphine.

Marge threw her hands up. "But how do you expect me to help you if I don't have all the facts? I'm working in the dark here, people!"

Delphine took a deep breath to calm herself. "Griffin, I'm hoping you can do us a favor."

Griffin sat up straighter. "I'm listening."

"Could you have Miko provide us with a list of current guests? I'd like to take a look at the names of everyone who booked a reservation for last week and this coming week."

"I don't have to ask him," Griffin said. "I have access to the reservation system and can go get you a list right now."

"That would be great!" said Kenji.

"No," said Delphine.

"Why not?" asked Griffin.

Delphine said, "It would be bad form to do so without informing Miko. He's your boss right now, for all intents and purposes. He may not have the power to fire you, but I guarantee you he's reporting to Fausto about how you're doing. You're in a probationary period. Once they see what your character is, they'll find you a permanent position. So just ask him. He'll say yes, and you'll be doing the right thing."

"You sound pretty sure," said Griffin.

Delphine nodded. "Now, if you don't mind, we really need that list."

Griffin stood up and placed her napkin on her plate. "I'm on it."

She left to find Miko, and Delphine put a few more appetizers on her plate.

"Now she's gone, you can fill me in," Marge said to Kenji.

"On what?" he asked.

"On what kind of consulting you did. I agree it was better not to tell Griffy, since she's a young person, and you know how they are with keeping secrets and whatnot. Plus she's kind of sensitive and impressionable or whatever. But she's not here, so you can tell me."

Kenji looked to Delphine for help, but Delphine turned her head. *She* wasn't going to be the one to do it. He was on his own.

He yawned and said, "Oh my, I am very tired. I think I need a nap. Super Babe, do you want to come?"

Marge gave him a dark scowl. "I don't think so," she said. "Have a good … nap."

"Thank you," he said in a tentative tone. He got up from the table, bowed, and disappeared.

Delphine hung her head. She knew what was coming.

"Okay, spill it," said Marge.

CHAPTER 21

"Spill what?" asked Delphine. The words sounded innocent enough, but Marge knew it was all an act. Delphine was never as naive as she pretended to be.

Well, Marge wasn't going to let her get away with it this time. Her frustration at being left out of whispered conversations and meaningful glances had built up to a point where she was ready to explode like a Hawaiian volcano.

"Why won't anyone tell me what's really going on, and what you used to do together?" said Marge, letting her hurt show. "I know you and Kenji have been friends for a long time. But why does it always feel like you have something to hide? I try to ignore your special little secret two-person club most of the time, but it's getting to be near impossible. And I don't think I want to play along anymore." She sat back and crossed her arms.

Delphine stayed quiet for a moment. Marge waited.

"Well," said Delphine. "It's not my story to tell, but—"

"See! All I get is excuses!" said Marge, only a few decibels below a bellow.

Delphine took a deep breath. "Kenji and I were involved in some dangerous things. He really cares for you. Dare I say, he loves you. But he doesn't want you to get hurt if something from his past comes back to bite him."

"Did you say … love?" said Marge. Her heart fluttered in her chest.

"Well, he hasn't told me in so many words—I'm sure you'll be the first person he'll say it to. But I've seen the way he looks at you. And I've never seen him act this way before."

"What way?" asked Marge, smiling.

"Like a lovestruck puppy," said Delphine.

Marge knew for a fact Delphine didn't like to use mushy words, so for her to break out a gem like *lovestruck* had to be a good sign.

"Awwwwww," said Marge as her eyes began to glisten with tears. "How sweet! And of course, I love him too."

"I know you do," said Delphine. "So be patient with him. He needs to tell you about it all in his own time. He's doing the best he can."

"Does the laptop have anything to do with all that stuff?" Marge ran a shrimp through a dollop of cocktail sauce on her plate and popped it in her mouth.

"I honestly don't know yet. But we're trying to find out. Do you think you could help us solve the mystery, yet be patient about not knowing all the details right now?"

Marge gazed up at the sky as she considered her friend's request. Her Kenji Bear loved her! Oh gosh, and she felt the same for him. And people in love made concessions, right? Compromises. For the greater good.

"No," she said.

"What? Why not?" Delphine sounded dumbfounded.

"Because I have been a patient girlfriend for a really long time now, and—"

"Please. You've been dating Kenji for six weeks," said Delphine.

"Okay but it feels like eons because we are soulmates. And

I've asked both of you repeatedly for information but all I get are lies and redirections. How can I help if I only know part of the story? It's a ridiculous request." She waved a hand at Delphine, brushing off the idea.

"Griffin agreed to help without knowing the whole story," Delphine pointed out.

"Oh brother," said Marge. "You always turn everything into an argument."

"Me?"

"Yeah, you," snapped Marge. "You think I'm not on to your tactics, but I got you figured out."

Delphine remained silent and Marge felt herself winning … whatever this was.

"But Kenji needs your help," said Delphine, trying one more time to appeal to logic.

But Marge was beyond logic. She resided in her emotions, which currently ran on the hot side. Oh who was she kidding, she ran hot most of the time. "Kenji will have to ask me himself, and he'll have to give me more info. Otherwise, no dice."

"I see," said Delphine. "How unfortunate."

"Kenji needs to learn I mean business," said Marge.

Now Delphine laughed. "I think we all know you mean business."

"What's that supposed to—you know what? Never mind. I'll prove it to both of you. As of right now, I am officially your roommate again."

Delphine, who had been about to put a forkful of food in her mouth, froze. "No."

"Oh yes."

"No. I won't allow it."

"You don't have a choice," said Marge. "I was your roommate first. So now it's like I never left. I can move back in because it was our original agreement."

"Can I take this opportunity to point out your logic makes absolutely no sense?"

"No, you cannot."

Marge watched as Delphine seemed to deflate right in front of her eyes.

"Come on, it'll be fun, us gals doing gal things together, like two swingin' singles," said Marge, feeling less joviality than her words implied.

"But you're not a swinging single," Delphine pointed out. "You have a very serious boyfriend."

"How about for a little while, we pretend I don't?" It would teach Kenji a lesson, thought Marge.

They sat there in silence and the warm ocean breeze picked up, reminding Marge she was in paradise for heaven's sake, and she should be having more fun than this. She wanted to forget all the arguing and the dumb laptop and go swimming. And she certainly didn't want to tell Delphine there was a second reason for moving out of Kenji's room.

Truth be told, she wasn't ready to shack up with her boyfriend quite yet. When Kenji had suggested they share a room, she'd thought she was prepared to take their relationship to a new place, but now they were here, something about the arrangement didn't feel right. Not because she didn't love him! But maybe because she did love him. And she felt a little embarrassed for not having been honest with herself sooner. Maybe picking this fight with Delphine and Kenji had been deflection. Perhaps she needed to be more forthcoming about her fear.

Then she decided, screw it! What they didn't know wouldn't hurt them for a little while longer, and in the meantime, she would take some time to figure out her feelings. Eventually, everything would work out fine. Just not right now.

"I'm moving back in with you tonight," said Marge. "Say, are you okay?" Delphine had started to turn pale.

"No," said Delphine.

"No biggie, if you don't feel good, I can get a porter to help me move my stuff. You take it easy."

Delphine pushed her plate away. "Great."

Marge frowned. "There is one thing I kinda regret."

"What?" asked Delphine. "Or maybe I don't want to know."

"I feel really bad about stealing Kenji's phone." Marge reached into the V-neck of her jumpsuit and pulled Kenji's cell phone out of her bra.

"I feel bad about you doing that too," said Delphine.

CHAPTER 22

Marge and Delphine sat and stared at Kenji's phone resting on the table between them like they were waiting for it to start levitating.

"I didn't want him to lose it somewhere, so when he got up to leave, I just, um, put it in a safe place," said Marge. It had seemed like a good idea to snatch it away at the time, but now it did feel a tiny bit like stealing.

Delphine's face wore a disapproving expression that made Marge feel even more guilty.

"What! He is always leaving his tech stuff all over the place! If his laptop hadn't gotten stolen, he probably would've lost it."

"It's plausible," said Delphine. "Maybe you can go take it to him right now."

"Why Delphine, are you wanting to get rid of me?" Marge gave her a wide smile.

"I don't think you really want me to answer that," said Delphine.

Marge picked up the phone and absentmindedly typed in Kenji's password. The phone popped open to the text from the laptop kidnappers. Her brow furrowed. "What's this about a girlfriend? How do they know what I used to do for a living?"

"What *did* you used to do?" asked Delphine.

"Now you're trying to change the subject."

"No, I'm curious. We haven't exactly been close friends over the years, I guess we've never talked about it."

"No, we haven't. And we haven't ever talked about what you did either. So we're even." But how did these thieves know what she used to do? Suddenly her stomach dropped to her feet. "You don't think they mean the Blingsters, do you?" she whispered to Delphine.

Delphine seemed to think about this. "I don't think so," she said after a moment. "You can't really tell what they mean or who they're referring to, based on context of the rest of their message."

"It means a lot if they know I'm a—if they know about what I almost got in trouble for," said Marge, putting Kenji's phone back on the table. "Maybe instead of Kenji's past getting me in trouble, mine might be causing *him* trouble."

Delphine reached out and put a hand on hers. "The thing is, Marge…"

Marge's something-bad-is-about-to-come-out-of Delphine's-mouth alarm went off.

"I think the laptop thieves might think I'm his girlfriend," said Delphine.

"Excuse me?" shouted Marge.

"There's a perfectly reasonable explanation."

Marge tapped her foot under the table. "I'm waiting."

Delphine had her open the text again and they read it together. "See, there." She pointed to the phone. "'We know what you both used to do.' It's as if they know Kenji and I used to work together."

"I think that's a stretch," said Marge. "The message could also mean they know I used to be a Blingster."

"Hmm," said Delphine.

"In any case, if they mean you, you must be giving them some reason to think you're his girl. Are you stepping out with my Kenji Bear behind my back?"

Delphine scoffed. "Don't be ridiculous."

"Why? You just spent a whole lot of energy trying to convince me of how great he is. So I know you like him."

"Of course I like him, he's my best friend. I also just spent a lot of energy trying to convince you he loves you," countered Delphine.

"Oh," said Marge. "True."

"However, if you think I might be after your Kenji Bear, perhaps you should stay in his room with him. You know, to keep an eye on him. You don't want to be my roommate, you're far too mad at me."

"Au contraire, mon roommate," said Marge. "I think you're the one I need to keep an eye on." She stood up and put Kenji's phone in her purse. "I've had enough of this weird conversation. I'm going to arrange for someone to move my things. After I take a swim."

Without waiting to see if Delphine would stop her (she knew Delphine wouldn't stop her), Marge marched to the pool and put her things down on a lounge chair. She took off her sandals and her swim cover-up, which Kenji had given back to her earlier. Funny, she didn't remember losing it in the first place, but oh well. Marge jumped into the pool. The refreshing salt water cooled her hot temper.

After swimming a few laps and splashing around in the shallow end, Marge got back out and laid down on a towel on her chair.

A club employee came over and asked if she needed anything. His name tag read *WENDELL*. Sadly for him, he looked like a Wendell. Kind of squishy and indoorsy—and he even wore thick-lensed glasses. He seemed out of place lit by sunshine.

"I guess I am still kinda peckish," said Marge. "What do you recommend as a midafternoon snacky-snack?"

"I'll bring you our organic farm-to-table cheese and fruit sampler," said Wendell. "And an iced coffee."

"Perfecto!" said Marge.

Wendell left to get her food. A few people splashed in the pool, and laughter came from the bar area. She glanced in that direction, on the off-chance Brock Celery might be around. But she didn't see him anywhere.

She settled back into her chair to enjoy the peaceful afternoon and not think about Kenji or Delphine or a missing computer.

But it was hard. She was still a little mad. Kenji and Delphine had their secret club and Marge always felt left out. Why did she feel like a third wheel when she was the girlfriend? She hoped Brock Celery would happen by, and she even sort of wished Kenji could see her talk to a movie star.

Marge didn't have to wait long to get the first part of her wish granted. Brock Celery sat down in the chair next to hers, wearing a salmon-pink T-shirt and light-blue shorts. He came across as so sporty and outdoorsy—the opposite of poor Wendell.

"Hi Marge," said Brock. He made her name sound like an exotic, fragrant herb.

"Hi Mr. Celery," said Marge with a level of formality she usually reserved for well, movie stars.

"Please, babe, call me Brock." He winked at her.

Wendell arrived with the cheese and fruit sampler and placed it on the small table between Marge and Brock's chairs.

"I'll be back with your iced coffee, ma'am," said Wendell. "Anything for you, Mr. Celery?"

"Iced coffee sounds scrumptious," said Brock, not taking his eyes off Marge. He raised an eyebrow and suddenly Marge felt vulnerable. She reached for a second towel to cover herself up with.

"Um, okay," said Wendell. He walked away.

"Is that the farm-to-table fruit and cheese sampler?" Brock asked. Without waiting for an answer, he leaned over and picked up a grape. He popped it in his mouth and chewed slowly and ogled Marge.

"Uh-huh," said Marge, strangely tongue-tied. Something about his chewing mesmerized her.

"I'm glad I found you," he said.

"You are?" Marge put a piece of cheese on a cracker and nibbled at it.

"I sure am," said Brock. "I've been thinking about you."

"Oh," she said, surprised. She couldn't think of what to follow up her brilliant response with. "Where's your manager?"

"He's getting a massage."

"Do they give good massages at the spa? I was thinking of going to get one."

Brock laughed. "Heck, I don't know. I don't go to spas, so I really don't care."

"How come you don't get massages?" Marge asked. "Everybody likes massages."

"I get massages, I just prefer to get them at home, from my lady friends." He wiggled his eyebrows at her. "If you know what I mean."

Marge tried to ignore the cringey statement because of who had said it. After all, she was sitting by a pool at an exclusive club with Brock Celery! If only Big El, Smitty, and Laverne could see her now. But Marge was pretty sure all the Blingsters were still in prison.

They ate more of the cheese and fruit, and Wendell brought iced coffees. Marge asked Brock questions about her favorite movie of his, *Forty Japanese Chickens*. It was about a woman who found out her husband had been cheating on him, so she exacts revenge by leaving forty Japanese Ukokkei chickens in their kitchen before taking off with her own new lover for a fun new life. Brock had played the adventurous new lover, of course. Marge wanted to know if the rumors were true about Brock having a real-life affair with the film's star, but he never gave her an actual answer.

Brock asked Marge about her love life. After a few attempts at trying to suggest she might have a boyfriend without coming right out and saying she had a boyfriend, Marge felt another strange sensation in her stomach. It was one she hadn't experienced very often. It felt a little like she might be in over her head.

"So I have a question for you Marge," said Brock, making her name sound herbal again.

"Yes?" she said.

His snow-white teeth appeared in a wide smile. "I'm glad you're agreeing, but don't you want to know what you've said yes to?"

"I didn't—I meant yes, I'm ready to hear your—I want to know what… Okay," said Marge.

"Have dinner with me tonight," said Brock. "I'll be over at seven. My personal chef, Stanislav, will cook something in the restaurant kitchen for us and bring it to your room."

"Why can't I come to your suite?" asked Marge.

Brock stood up. "Perfect! I can't wait to be alone with you, Marge. What's your room number?"

Her stomach tightened. She should say no thank you. She should tell him she had a real nice boyfriend. She should tell him she didn't eat food cooked by people named Stanislav. She should tell him anything other than a room number. The man was trouble. On the other hand, the man was Brock Celery. Marge knew a dozen women who would kill to be in her shoes. If she'd been wearing any.

"Room number, babe," said Brock Celery.

"202." It left her mouth of its own volition.

"Fantastic. See you later." Brock Celery sauntered away. He looked back at her and smiled and disappeared into the men's locker room.

CHAPTER 23

Kenji had desperately needed a nap. But as soon as he'd laid his head on the pillow of the luxurious bed in his and Marge's hotel room, he knew a nap would remain nothing more than an abstract theory. Too many thoughts swirled through his mind and made sleep impossible.

And to add insult to injury, an hour later, Marge had showed up and informed him she was moving out of their room. She insisted she couldn't sleep in the same bed as someone who wasn't totally honest with her. When he'd remained silent, still determined to protect his sweetie from his own questionable and sometimes violent past, she proceeded to pack up her things.

She'd returned his phone to him, pointing out the tiny detail from the thieves' text about the girlfriend stuff, and asked him if it referred to Delphine or herself. Kenji didn't have an answer for her. He'd been so distraught he hadn't even thought to ask why his Super Babe had his phone in the first place. Then she'd left, saying she'd be back in the evening to get her bags.

He felt like he might melt away into nothingness, such was his despair. He'd wanted this trip to be perfect for the two of them. Now it was anything but.

Kenji sat at a small, shaded table on the beach in front of the resort. Delphine strolled up and joined him.

"Griffin and Miko should be here any minute," she said. "You look terrible, by the way."

"I feel terrible." He wanted to lie down in the sand and cry. But hopefully Griffin would have good news for them. Or just some plain old news would be nice too, at this point. "Where is Marge, do you know?"

"if I'm not mistaken, she went to get a massage at the spa."

Kenji shook his head. He had wanted to surprise her with a couples massage, but it didn't seem likely that would happen now.

"Did she tell you she's moving to my room?" Delphine asked.

Kenji sighed.

"Don't worry. We'll sort it all out." She patted him on the forearm.

"You know, I am not sure I need or want any more of your help in sorting out my romantic life," he said.

"Perfect," said Delphine, unfazed by what should have been taken as an insult. "More time for me to relax."

Kenji sighed again. Nuts.

"Sorry we're late," said Griffin, sitting down at the table with them. "Is it okay if Miko is here?"

"Of course," said Delphine.

"He used to work for the CIA, did you know that?" asked Griffin. "Oh, but how could you know, he just told me."

"I did know, yes," said Delphine.

Miko sat down next to Delphine and turned to Griffin with a stunned expression on his face. "You're right, she really does know everything."

"It's not as helpful as you would think," said Kenji.

"Okay," said Griffin, "but do you know what he used to do at the CIA?"

"Yes, and I know why he left." Delphine put a hand on Miko's arm. "But I won't tell anyone."

"So about that list," said Kenji.

Griffin handed him a manila folder. "Here's a list of everyone at the resort as of today. Plus lists for last week's and next week's reservations. Oh, and I also included the names of people who have access to the club."

"Good thinking," said Kenji. "Thank you."

"The list doesn't have room numbers though," said Miko. "But if you find a name you want us to check, we can."

"This should be good enough to bet us started," said Delphine.

Kenji gave Delphine a few lists. "Let us see if any names jog a memory or seem familiar."

"Right." She took two pens out of her purse and handed one to Kenji, and they started checking names.

While they read, Griffin and Miko compared stories about working for the government.

Five minutes later, Kenji and Delphine exchanged lists. She'd put checkmarks next to a few names, as had he. When they finished, they had ten names identified.

He collected all the papers. "Some of them I wasn't sure about," he said. "Let me restate myself. I am not sure about any names on these lists, but few feel familiar somehow."

"I thought the same thing," said Delphine. "And how inconvenient—we can't do the research, because you don't have your laptop."

"Yes Delphine, the irony is not lost on me." He ran his hand through his hair. "I suppose I will have to call the office and ask my new boss to check these names for us."

"Who took Richard Dere's place?" asked Delphine. "I've been wondering, but at the same time haven't cared enough to ask."

"Someone named Irene Roquefort, if you can believe it," said Kenji.

Delphine chuckled.

"Why is that funny?" asked Griffin.

Delphine sighed. "You would have to be a French cheese aficionado to understand."

"IYKYK, right?" asked Miko, grinning. Griffin laughed.

"What?" said Kenji.

"If you know, you know," said Griffin.

"I do not know, so I guess I do not know," said Kenji, in no mood for deciphering hipster jargon.

"Moving on," said Delphine. "You can't ask Roquefort. You said you brought your laptop on this trip because you had some work to do. If you go asking for help with something you should be able to do yourself, she's going to know you don't have your computer. It'll raise a big red flag."

"Oh shoot, you are right," said Kenji. "We are screwed."

"Well, I can't help," said Griffin. "I don't know anyone at the FBI anymore."

Delphine looked thoughtful for a moment, then said, "I'll call Judy again."

"Again?" Kenji asked.

"Oh," said Delphine. "Right. Well, I called her earlier to ask her to check up on someone. This time I'll tell her I owe her an even bigger favor." She turned to Griffin. "Judy is someone we know at our old field office. She's a friend and won't mind doing a little legwork for us."

Griffin nodded. "What can Miko and I do?"

"Keep your cell phone handy," said Kenji, "in case we need you in a hurry."

He was sad he wouldn't get to do the research himself; he'd always enjoyed sifting through family histories, credit reports, and psychological profiles. He'd been good at the physical aspects of his old job too, and liked all the fighting and high-speed chases. But his computer-nerd side loved the tedious fact-finding tasks, which was one of the main reasons he'd signed on for the part-time consulting gig in the first place. The very one that had now landed him in so much hot water, both professionally and personally.

CHAPTER 24

Griffin and Miko said their goodbyes and left; they were headed back to the Conte estate for the rest of the day. Apparently Miko lived in a small bungalow near the main mansion, and Fausto had provided Griffin with a cozy apartment above his on-site sound studio. The arrangement sounded like a lovely setup to Delphine, it being in a tropical paradise and all. She hoped to see Griffin's place before her vacation ended.

But first they had to deal with Kenji's blasted laptop.

Delphine dialed Judy's cell, put her phone on speaker, and laid it on the table. She and Kenji hunched over the device as Judy answered. Delphine explained what they needed, and Judy agreed to help them out. Delphine agreed to text the list of names when she hung up, and Judy promised to call back as soon as she could.

"What should we do in the meantime?" asked Kenji after Delphine had sent the list.

"You could go try to win Marge back," Delphine suggested.

"No," said Kenji.

He was hedging. "Why not?" Delphine asked.

"I need to give her some time. Maybe it is better if we are apart for a little while."

"Let me guess. You were really looking forward to this romantic vacation with your lady friend, but when it came right down to it, you realized you weren't quite ready to take the step you thought you were ready to take."

Kenji's jaw dropped. "How did you know?"

Delphine huffed. She didn't want to tell him his girlfriend was most likely feeling the same way. Marge hadn't come right out and said it, but the woman was always more transparent than she realized. In any case it wasn't her place to say anything.

"Either I'm a relationship genius, or you're totally open book," she said.

"Probably a little of both," said Kenji.

"I've also known you a very long time," she reminded him.

"I just think the physical part of a relationship is very special," said Kenji. "I do not want to take it for granted. I thought I would be okay with it, but I want to show Marge more respect than that."

"That's very admirable of you," said Delphine.

"You don't think I am a prude?"

She shook her head. "I think you are a gentleman."

Delphine suggested they go to the restaurant at the club, but Kenji said he didn't want to risk running into Marge. So they decided to try one of the smaller eateries within the resort. The settled on the closest one—a little place that served ramen and other Japanese foods. It wasn't as fancy as the restaurant at the club, but it still had a nice view of the bay. They ordered green tea and made small talk while they waited for Judy to call back.

After their second cup of tea, Delphine's phone rang. Judy had some information for them. Delphine put the phone on speaker, since no one else was seated in the outdoor area near them.

"I cross-checked your list with a few of our databases," said Judy. "Ran all the names through, not only the ones you checked off. I didn't get any direct matches."

"Darnit," said Kenji. "Well, we are screwed."

"But I might have found something else," she added.

Delphine flashed Kenji a scowl for having spoken too soon. "Like what?"

"I found two names similar to a couple on your list. I've sent you an email with some information you can look over."

"Thank you so much Judy," said Delphine. "I can't tell you how much I appreciate your help. And your confidentiality."

"I'm just grateful you got rid of Dere for us," said Judy. "He was a horrible human being."

"Is your new manager any better?" asked Delphine.

"Too soon to tell," said Judy. Kenji nodded his agreement.

"Let's have lunch soon to catch up," Delphine said into her phone.

"I'd like that," said Judy.

As soon as she hung up the call, Delphine navigated through her apps and opened her email. A new message from Judy sat at the top of her inbox.

"I wish we could see this on a bigger screen," said Kenji.

She scowled at him again.

"Oh, sorry."

Judy sent a PDF file, three pages long. It was a summary of information on a Norwegian couple, Olafur and Lilja Solberg.

"Do those names sound familiar to you?" Delphine asked Kenji.

"No," said Kenji.

Delphine started to read the document in a quiet voice to Kenji. "They seemed to be part of..."

Kenji leaned in closer. "Of what?"

"They were bagmen for the Herring Mafia."

"Ohhhhh." He leaned back in his chair again. "Where did they live?"

"Ballangen."

"That is near..."

"Narvik, yes."

The town they'd gotten stuck in. The town where everything had gone wrong.

Delphine continued to read the document. "Olafur and Lilja were associated with the Herring Mafia around the same time we were in Norway," she said, summarizing. She and Kenji and the rest of her team had been there to take down the Fish Boss, a Norwegian criminal by the name of Gunnar "Fish Guts" Hovland.

"Do you remember the mission?" Delphine asked.

"How could I forget," said Kenji. "I think that one was our biggest failure."

Which was the short way of saying lives had been lost, and they hadn't accomplished their goal. Fish Guts and his henchmen had found out about Delphine and her crew and tried to have them eliminated. A shootout had occurred. She'd lost one team member, and the Herring Mafia had lost at least four.

"What else does it say?" asked Kenji, pointing to her phone.

She scanned the rest of the pages. "Let's see. Oh. They died while we were in Narvik. The official cause of death is listed as tainted herring."

"Actual cause of death?" asked Kenji.

"Bullets."

"The shootout at the grocery store," said Kenji in a distant-sounding voice.

Delphine shivered. If they wanted to, they could easily sit there all afternoon drinking tea and reliving their last Norwegian mission; it would've been a great jumping-off point to examine all their other failures too. Granted, their success rate had been very high, but you couldn't win them all, as the saying went. Or in this case, þú getur ekki unnið þá alla.

Delphine scrolled to the next page in the PDF and found black-and-white photos of Olafur and Lilja. She positioned the phone so Kenji could study the faces of the two mafia members with her. Olafur's hair seemed very blond, and he a round face. Lilja's hair was dark and her face slender. A handsome couple, if you overlooked their association with the Herring Mafia.

"So what is the connection to the laptop?" Kenji asked.

"This says Olafur and Lilja left behind two young children." Delphine pulled the hotel and club guest lists from her purse and ran a finger down the first page. Then the second. On the fourth, she hit paydirt. "Minka and Martin Solberg are hotel guests. They got here yesterday like we did."

Kenji's eyes went wide with surprise. So did Delphine's.

"Is there a photo of the children in the original file?" He tried to look at the phone screen.

Delphine slid the device over to him so he could see. "No, only of the parents. In any case, they're not children anymore. They'd be in their forties by now. But I bet Miko can find us a room number, and maybe some video footage too."

"What if they think we killed their parents?" Kenji asked, wringing his hands.

"We kind of did, in a roundabout way," said Delphine.

"You can plan and plan, but there is always the risk of collateral damage."

"Try telling that to two kids who lost their parents in a produce-section shootout."

Kenji bent over. "My stomach hurts."

She patted his back. "Mine too. But here we are."

"Yes, but how in the world did they know we were here, or connect us to the deaths?"

Delphine sighed. "We don't have enough information to know."

Kenji sat up straight again. "Do you ever feel like we read too much into things? Like maybe our imaginations get the better of us, after all these years? Maybe we are imagining all this backstory."

"Sure," said Delphine. "But isn't that a potentially dangerous assumption to make?"

"Yes," admitted Kenji. "I don't think ignoring the data is a chance I am willing to take. Let's call Miko now. Because if these people think we killed their parents…"

Delphine nodded. "They might be after whole lot more than ransom money."

"Revenge," they said at the same time.

CHAPTER 25

Delphine's mind raced. Memories mixed with current events, and all of it had become tainted by the possibility of retribution much greater than the loss of two million dollars. She needed to have some time alone to think, so after they called Miko to ask him to a get room number and photos of the Solberg siblings, she and Kenji parted at the restaurant to go their rooms to rest. They planned to meet back up once they had more information.

The possible connection to the past had brought up so many questions for Delphine. What were the odds the Solberg siblings just happened to be on a Hawaiian vacation at the same time as her and Kenji? How did the children know so much about her and Kenji's past? Were they still part of the Herring Mafia? If that were the case, she and Kenji were in even *more* trouble. Delphine quickened her pace as she wound her way through the resort.

As she turned a corner and came upon the swimming pool—the one where she had turned down a date with Kapuni Jones—the sound of laughter caught her attention. The laugh sounded familiar. She crouched behind a large grouping of Maile-scented ferns and clocked three figures standing together in the shade of the pool house, talking.

One of them faced her. Kapuni Jones. His thin frame shook as he laughed again. She wished he was alone, and she could go talk to him. Just to say hello, mind you. Not because he was interesting or had a nice laugh.

The other two people, a man and a woman, stood with their backs to Delphine. The man had hair so blond it looked white. The woman wore a hat, but her shoulder-length dark hair was easy to spot.

"I love pineapples!" said Kapuni. The other two people laughed.

Delphine pursed her lips. Could it be Martin and Minka standing there? How ridiculous. She was now so preoccupied by thoughts of Norway and Fish Mafias and past events she was starting to read too much into things, as Kenji had feared.

But maybe it wasn't a far-fetched conclusion to draw. She needed to investigate.

Delphine stayed behind the ferns as Kapuni and the two other people left the shade of the pool house and made their way out of the gated area. Kapuni offered them a cordial goodbye and walked away in the direction of the club. Delphine thought she might be able to overhear the man and woman talking to each other—in Norwegian, perhaps?—but they turned to go in the opposite direction without saying a word.

When they were about fifteen yards down the path, Delphine slowly unfolded herself from behind the ferns. Her goal was to catch a glimpse of their faces, so she decided to follow them. The two figures continued down the walkway, headed for the far end of the resort. It was then Delphine noticed the ink on the woman's left calf.

The tattoo was small line drawing of a fishing boat done in black ink. The same design printed on the calling card left by the laptop thieves. She clenched her fists and unclenched them again as she remembered where she'd seen the graphic before: tattooed on the arm of the Fish Boss, Fish Guts Hovland. Or to be more specific—in a photo of Fish Guts's dead body they'd seen in a debriefing file a few years after the disastrous Narvik mission.

Fish Guts had met with an untimely end when the boss of an Eastern European smelt gang finally did what Delphine and her crew hadn't managed to pull off.

The siblings had walked farther down the path. Delphine was just about to start take a step—

"There you are!" barked Marge, and she took hold of Delphine's arm.

Delphine jumped with surprise. But her shock turned to anger. Honestly, she could wring Marge's neck sometimes. How did her friend always have the worst timing!

"Hey, you look kind of mad," said Marge.

"You're very astute," said Delphine. She chanced a glance down the pathway in time to see the man and woman turn in her direction. Marge's booming voice must've caught their attention. It was the worst possible thing that could've happened, and Delphine had about a half second to do something about it.

She wrenched herself free from Marge's grasp, wrapped both her arms around her friend, and hugged her. She leaned in so her lips came close to Marge's.

Marge tried to lean back. "Why Big D, this is a new development."

Delphine released her hug but kept Marge close. She interlaced arms with Marge and they strolled down the path away from the two figures. Delphine laid her head on Marge's shoulder. "Follow my lead," she whispered.

"Okay," Marge whispered back. "You know, this explains a lot about the two maintenance ladies on your balcony this morning. I told Kenji you were cutting loose!"

"What?" said Delphine.

"I'm really flattered, but you should know I just don't swing that way."

"Keep walking with me and for god's sake, don't look back." Delphine prayed for once Marge would do as instructed.

Fortunately, she did.

CHAPTER 26

When they'd walked for several minutes, Delphine slowed down and let go of Marge's arm.

"So are you gonna explain what just happened?" asked Marge.

"Not right now," said Delphine.

Marge stopped in her tracks. "See, this is what I'm talking about. You and Kenji are all, 'Marge, do this, Marge, do that. Marge, let's make out in the bushes.' But no one ever tells me why."

Some days, Delphine wanted to bop Marge on the head with a lounge chair. She pulled on Marge's arm, and they started walking again. "You're one of my best friends but honestly, some days I don't have the energy to deal with you," she said.

Marge stopped again. "Did you say 'best friend?'"

Delphine gave her a blank stare. "I'm pretty sure I said 'one of.'"

Marge said, "No, you said I'm your best friend!"

"I definitely did not say that. And if I did happen to misspeak, this conversation is pushing you way down the list," said Delphine.

"No, you said it! No backsies, no backsies!" Marge laughed and so did Delphine.

It was hard to stay mad at her silly friend, thought Delphine. Sometimes.

They started off again and Marge said, "I was looking for you because I'm ready to move into your room."

In all the activity of the afternoon, Delphine had forgotten about getting a new roommate. "Oh," she said, not able to sound very excited.

"All my stuff is packed up, we just need to go get it and move it to your room."

Delphine sighed. She hadn't told anyone about her new suite for a reason—so she'd have something that was hers alone. But now the jig was up. "Okay, let's go get your things."

When they made it to room 204, Kenji wasn't there. Perhaps he'd stayed in the restaurant to have a little dinner, thought Delphine—it was about time to eat after all.

They stood on the landing, looking into the room.

"I really think you should stay and try to work things out with Kenji," Delphine said, trying one last time to hang onto her freedom.

"There's nothing to work out," said Marge.

"Oh but there is," said Delphine. "I mean, you two belong together. You can't leave things unresolved, and you certainly shouldn't sleep in different beds." A thin sheen of sweat surfaced on her palms. Her concern was less about the health of her friend's relationship, and more about losing the sanctity of her hotel suite. She felt bad about her selfishness ... for about five seconds.

"Nope, not gonna deal with it today. I'm kind of mad at you both, but us gals need to stick together."

"If you're mad at both of us, maybe you should get a room all to yourself," suggested Delphine.

"You're funny, Big D." Marge pointed to her three suitcases. "All this needs to go."

"I still don't understand why you needed to bring so much stuff," said Delphine. "We're only here for six days."

"I guess I'm not as unitarian as you," said Marge.

"Maybe you mean utilitarian?"

"I don't think so," said Marge. She pointed at the bags again. "Besides, we don't have to go very far with them."

Delphine remained silent as she rolled a suitcase onto the landing.

"Can't you take one more?" asked Marge, struggling to get the other two bags out the door.

"No," said Delphine. "I'm too unitarian."

They made it out onto the walkway and Marge tossed the keycard into the room and closed the door. She walked a few steps down the landing in the direction of room 202, and stopped when she noticed Delphine wasn't following. "Aren't you coming?"

"There's something I need to tell you," said Delphine.

"Oh brother," said Marge.

Ten minutes later, Delphine sat on one of the couches in her suite, watching Marge unpack a bag. Her fancy hotel suite felt much smaller than it had earlier in the day.

Marge disappeared into the bathroom with her toiletry bag and Delphine had visions of her new roomie's underthings draped all over the beautiful big space. She tried not to cry.

"I cannot believe you moved into this amazing suite and didn't tell me," Marge said, hanging up several jumpsuits in the closet.

"I don't tell you lots of things," said Delphine, watching her new roommate from one of the couches in the living room.

"Yeah, and that worries me," said Marge. She stood in the doorway between the bedroom and the living area. "You said I am your best friend. You should tell me everything."

"Do you tell me everything?" asked Delphine, and then she regretted it. The very last thing she wanted was for Marge to think she needed to talk more.

"No," said Marge. She lowered her head and walked to the couch like a third grader who had gotten picked last for a kickball team. She sat down right next to Delphine. "I'm sorry. I know I'm being kind of a pill."

"Kind of," said Delphine. She sighed. "Okay. You want me to tell you more? I'll tell you what I'm thinking."

Marge's head popped up in anticipation.

Delphine steepled her hands in her lap. "I think you're avoiding Kenji because you have commitment issues. You're afraid of getting too close to someone."

Marge looked at her for exactly one second and then burst into loud guffaws. She slapped Delphine on the shoulder so hard, Delphine almost fell off the couch. "Oh me oh my, that's the funniest thing I've heard in a long time!"

"I don't see why it's funny," said Delphine, offended.

Marge screeched with laughter and took deep gulps of air. "And that's why it's so … dang … hilarious!"

There was nothing for it but to sit back and wait until Marge finished with whatever sort of episode she was having. The pressure around Delphine's jaw increased. Not only was she stuck with a roommate in her single-lady's-dream hotel room, but she was being ridiculed by the silliest woman she'd ever met in her life.

Marge managed to catch her breath and wiped the tears from her eyes. "Honestly Delphine, for someone who thinks they're so smart, sometimes getting through to you is as hard as putting socks on a rooster."

Still Delphine stayed silent. Oftentimes, engaging Marge only made things worse.

"All I mean is, look who's talking, sister!" said Marge. "You never go on dates. Apparently the only man friend you have is my boyfriend. Can you blame me for thinking something might be up between you two? When was the last time someone checked under your hood?"

"Could you please not talk to me like I'm an automobile?" asked Delphine. But it was no use. Marge had hit the nail on the head. Had Delphine said no to a date with Kapuni Jones because she didn't trust him, or had she been afraid or unwilling to open herself up to someone else? Probably a little of both. She frowned. It annoyed her when Marge showed flashes of insight into the human psyche. It didn't happen often, but still. Although Marge wasn't dumb—not by a long stretch. Delphine didn't like to be pegged so easily by others, but she was probably more transparent than she intended.

She couldn't think of any snappy comebacks to Marge's digs.

Delphine stood up from the couch and went to the bar. Her first thought was to reach for the whiskey, but she changed her mind. She'd never been one to drink, and she wasn't going to let Marge drive her to it now, even though she'd never been so tempted in her life.

Marge stood also. "Anyhoo, It's too late now, and I'm staying here with you. This is a much nicer room! And if the last few months have taught us anything, it's that you and I make great roommates." She went back to the closet and hung up another jumpsuit next to Delphine's favorite linen blazer.

Again Delphine's mind was devoid of a reply. Besides, there probably wasn't much point in arguing.

CHAPTER 27

While Marge finished putting her things away, Delphine went out to the extended balcony and texted Griffin to ask whether they'd found anything on Minka and Martin Solberg. Griffin said she thought Miko hadn't found anything yet because a minor emergency had come up in the organic chicken coop at the estate, but he'd get to it as soon as he could.

Delphine pulled out the calling card the thieves had left behind. The fishing boat graphic had to connect them with the Herring Mafia. And it connected the man and woman Delphine saw talking to Kapuni with the whole thing too. It would make sense that those two figures had been Minka and Martin. If not, this thing was bigger than she'd thought and there could be at least four people at the resort associated with her and Kenji's past.

Five, if she counted Kapuni Jones.

Which she absolutely did.

She wished for once she could avoid seeing things through the eyes of a professional spy. But in this case, even a layperson could guess potential trouble lay around almost every corner, and that Kapuni Jones could not be trusted.

Delphine put the brakes on her thoughts, backed up, and took a different turn, away from the dark alley she'd been starting down. Why hadn't Minka and Martin's names shown up in Judy's databases? She texted her friend to ask, but Judy didn't reply.

Marge came out to join her holding two glasses of wine. She put them on the coffee table and sat on the couch opposite Delphine. Delphine didn't want wine, but Marge seemed sad, so she thanked her for the glass and took a sip.

"This is good, what is it?" she asked.

"I don't know. I told the room service people to send up their best stuff, pronto. And here we are." Marge took a long drink of her wine and smacked her lips. "Oh, it is pretty good, isn't it." She looked out at the bay, which was darkening as dusk settled on the island. She ran a hand over the couch cushion. "This is such a nice balcony. Way better than Kenji's."

"Yes, but this balcony is missing something," said Delphine.

"What's that?"

"Kenji."

Marge lifted one shoulder in a noncommittal gesture. "I guess." But Delphine could tell Marge missed her boyfriend.

"It's dinnertime," said Delphine. "Shall we call him and see what he's up to tonight?" Delphine didn't feel like going out, but she did feel like trying to find some way of getting Marge back into Kenji's room, and she wasn't above tagging along to play matchmaker.

"Nah," said Marge. "Can we just get something delivered?"

"Are you sure you want to spend a night in paradise shut up in a room with another old lady?" asked Delphine, desperate now.

"I'm sure."

Delphine didn't believe her. And something had to be wrong, because Marge hadn't given her a hard time about saying *another old lady*. "What's the problem?" she gestured at Marge to continue talking.

"I'm kinda trying to avoid someone," said Marge. "Not that you aren't great company! I know this is paradise, and it really is such a nice night, but—"

"Who are you trying to avoid?" asked Delphine.

Again, Marge's shoulder rose, and she gazed down at the outdoor carpet. "I might have maybe said yes to going on a date with someone."

"Let me guess," said Delphine.

"It's just that he's so hot! And super persuasive in person. He smiled, and before I knew what was happening, I'd agreed to a date. I literally could not say no."

"I'm sure," said Delphine. She doubted Brock Celery had to try very hard to get a yes out of Marge.

Marge let out a little laugh. "He would've made a great used car salesman."

Delphine had met her share of greasy actors who could pull one over on almost anybody. Except for the wonderful Pedro Bernal. She'd remember him fondly till her dying breath. And maybe even longer.

But Brock Celery? He fit in the used-car salesman category but tonight Delphine would not give Marge the favor of understanding. The woman had a boyfriend for heaven's sake. She crossed her arms and glared at Marge.

"Don't look at me like that. I said I'm not going," snapped Marge.

"You want extra points for being faithful?"

Marge huffed. "Never mind. My mistake, thinking you'd understand."

Delphine leaned forward to make her point. "Let's get something straight. You might be one of my best friends, but Kenji is my very best friend. And if you ever hurt my very best friend, I'll … I'll…" Delphine couldn't think of what she wanted to say. Actually she knew exactly what she wanted to say, but it was incredibly impolite and could perhaps be construed as threatening.

"I know," said Marge. "You'll make me regret it for the rest of my life."

Delphine leaned back again. "As long as we're clear."

Marge nodded.

"Great. Now let's order some dinner." Delphine went back inside to peruse the room service menu, and Marge followed a few seconds later like a scolded child.

"Shall we play some cards while we wait for our food?" asked Delphine.

"Actually, I want to take a bath. The tub in there is amazing," said Marge, hooking a thumb in the direction of the huge bathroom.

Marge went off for a bath and Delphine realized Judy had texted and so had Griffin. She went back on the balcony to see what was what.

Judy said that after a little more digging, she discovered all the files having to do with the Herring Mafia had been moved to a higher level of classification, which she didn't have access to. Which meant Delphine and Kenji would have to work without knowing the whole picture. A disadvantage, to be sure. She wondered if Kenji had access to those files. Then she wondered if they'd ever have a chance to find out. Delphine texted Judy back telling her thank you, and she'd be in touch if they needed anything else.

The text from Griffin was to both Delphine and Kenji, letting them know Miko would hopefully have photos and/or room numbers for the Solbergs the following day. A delay wasn't ideal, but espionage worked like that sometimes—hurry up and wait. Besides, she was too tired to do anything else for the day anyway.

A bellhop delivered their room service and Delphine sat at the dining table, still texting with Kenji and Griffin, when Marge finally came out of the bathroom.

"What are you doing?" asked Marge, sounding accusatory.

"I'm setting up something fun for tomorrow morning," said Delphine. "We're getting a tour of the bay on a charter boat, doesn't that sound nice?" She put her phone aside and lifted the cloche from her plate to reveal a beautiful green salad topped with all kinds of fresh vegetables and a big piece of grilled salmon.

Marge sat down in the chair opposite her. "Will Griffy be there?"

"Yes. I invited Miko to come too, but he's unable to join us." Delphine tried to sound peppy, hoping to get Marge excited about the excursion.

"And will Kenji be there?"

"He's coming too. Now, we need to get up early so we can get to the marina by nine. I thought we could try the breakfast buffet at the club's restaurant. I know how you love buffets."

Marge lifted the cloche on her dinner—a hamburger with sweet potato fries. "No. And I don't want to go on a boat tour."

"Well too bad. We're going. We have to talk with Kenji about what to do next." And when trying to mediate an argument, thought Delphine, it was always best to do so on neutral territory. "And it'll be fun to see more of the bay."

Marge grunted.

All through dinner Delphine worked hard to try to cheer up Marge, to no avail. It was exhausting work. By the time they were done it was late enough to be almost bedtime, and Delphine decided to take a bath before getting into her wonderfully comfortable bed.

Marge flopped on the couch and turned on the giant TV.

"If I'm not out of the bath by the time you want to go to sleep, remember the couch you're sitting on pulls out into a queen-sized bed."

"Okay," said Marge.

Delphine gathered her robe and nightgown and entered the bathroom. The tub was sparkling and dry—Marge must have cleaned it out after using it, which was very thoughtful. And she'd only left a bra and two swimsuits hanging from knobs around the room.

Delphine gave herself time to think about Kapuni Jones as she soaked in the tub. Truthfully, she was a little disappointed not to have run into him again after their nice lunch. She told herself it was because she wanted to grill him about the people he'd talked to by the pool house. But it also might have been because she'd enjoyed his company. And now she remembered one of the main reasons she avoided romance since she'd lost her darling Charles years ago. Relationships were confusing and hard and often resulted in conflicted feelings.

Delphine got out of the bath, dressed in her nightgown, and brushed her teeth. Things were silent out in the living room; Marge must've given up on TV and gone to sleep on the sofa bed. Delphine turned out the bathroom light and quietly opened the door.

And there was Marge, fast asleep in the very middle of Delphine's king-sized bed.

Delphine leaned over and nudged Marge. "Hey. Go sleep on the couch."

"Mrphlmrph," said Marge.

Delphine tried again, to no avail.

Well *she* certainly wasn't going to sleep on the couch, this was her room after all! She climbed into bed next to Marge. She flopped around and tugged on the blanket, and tried to be annoying as possible, but Marge didn't budge.

Delphine had to laugh. She never thought she'd be getting into bed with anyone again. And now that she had … it was with Marge Flanders.

CHAPTER 28

At 8:45 the next morning, Delphine and Marge met Kenji in the resort lobby, and they all took a shuttle van to Kaimoa Marina. The morning had been uneventful so far—no sign of a dark-haired woman with a tattoo on her calf and a man with very blond hair at the breakfast buffet, or anywhere else for that matter. Even so, Delphine would feel much better once they were on the boat and out in the bay.

Griffin was already waiting for them when the van arrived at the marina. Following the directions Miko had given Delphine, they walked along the maze of docks until they came to a sign for DuPree Charter Boats. Jimmy DuPree, a friend of Miko's, would be their captain on the morning cruise around Kaimoa Bay.

Jimmy DuPree took Delphine's hand and helped her into his boat.

"Thank you," she said. "It's nice to meet you, Jimmy."

"You're welcome, and it's nice to meet you too, ma'am." He let go of her hand and doffed an imaginary cap. "Any friend of Miko's is a friend of mine."

Jimmy was a huge young man; not exactly lean, but not obese either. Just … big. He must have played football, Delphine guessed. He had an open, friendly face and she knew they were in good hands.

"Miko told me you two met in college," she said.

"Correct. Cal State Long Beach. Hooooo! Feels like a million years ago now."

Delphine frowned at him. "Tell me about it."

Marge and Griffin had already boarded and were looking around the charter boat, which was a forty-footer in very nice condition. Jimmy had installed a diving platform off the stern, and a lot of comfortable seating along the sides of the boat.

Kenji came over to stand next to Delphine. "I feel like we should be doing something more constructive than riding around on a boat," he said.

"Maybe it's okay to relax for a few minutes," said Delphine.

"I am too stressed out," said Kenji, rubbing his stomach.

"I know," said Delphine, and put a hand on his arm. She glanced in Marge's direction. Marge glared at her, and her eyes moved to Delphine's hand on Kenji's shoulder. Delphine removed her hand.

"We are supposed to meet these people tomorrow, and we have not heard from them."

"They want their money, so we'll hear from them,"

"Okay, but I have an even bigger problem now," said Kenji. Instead of rubbing his stomach he now clutched at it.

"Please tell me how all of this is now worse," said Delphine.

Kenji sighed. "Frances called me last night. She cannot liquidate my crypto money."

Now Delphine's stomach hurt too. "Why not? Oh never mind, it doesn't matter, does it."

"The market is in freefall right now," Kenji explained. "I put a lot of money into a memecoin and it is tanking. It might have been a pump and dump situation, or a rug pull. You see, I read online about—"

"I have no idea what you're talking about," said Delphine. "And before you start drawing me charts or whatever, just don't."

She looked out at the water but was lost in thought and didn't really see it. "This information does present a few new challenges, doesn't it."

"Yes. I made a few more calls to see if I could get the cash from anywhere else, but it is too late now. I can't do it by tomorrow."

"Okay," said Delphine.

"It is?" asked Kenji.

"No, but it's not the end of the world either. We simply have to think of a way to get around this latest development."

"I have been trying," said Kenji. "I didn't get any sleep last night. We are supposed to meet with these people tomorrow, Delphine, and I have nothing."

Delphine reached out to put her hand on Kenji's arm again but stopped herself at the last second. The last thing they all needed was for things to blow up even more between Kenji and his girlfriend. "Let's try to enjoy the next few hours, okay? And why not use this time to reconnect with Marge? You can't keep avoiding each other on your romantic getaway vacation."

Kenji moaned and held his stomach again. "Do you think we are safe out here on this boat?"

"I thought about that, and I believe so. There's strength in numbers, as they say, so I figure if all of us are together, things should be fine."

"I don't know," said Kenji.

She sighed heavily. "I never should have invited you and Marge on this trip. All I wanted was a nice, quiet vacation. And now look at us." She sounded angry, because she was. No one wanted to go on vacation and have to try harder than usual not to get killed. It was always a real downer.

Kenji snorted. "Like you could keep a Hawaiian vacation secret from Marge."

Sometimes she hated it when he was somewhat right.

"Besides, I think you would have been bored if we were not here to keep you company and make things interesting."

She really hated it when he was almost spot-on. "Pish," she said.

Jimmy gave his guests a quick tour of the boat, showing them the location of the bathroom, the bow seating, and most importantly, the snacks.

"Can we use your big mythical beast?" asked Kenji.

Jimmy's eyebrows rose. "Excuse me?"

Kenji pointed to what appeared to be a large unicorn inflatable tied with rope to the boat's railing outside the main cabin.

Jimmy laughed. "Oh! That's my niece's. I'm taking them out for a sunset swim later and she told me she'd disown me as her uncle if I didn't bring it. I guess you could, if you don't destroy it."

Marge huffed. "Kenji, you're all serious and mature and stuff on the surface, but underneath you're still a little kid." Her voice sounded disappointed and reprimanding.

"But I thought those are the kinds of things you liked about me." Kenji put a hand on his heart as if he'd been mortally wounded.

"Hmph," said Marge. "Sometimes a little maturity is the better way to go."

Kenji looked like he might cry and went to stand next to the giant Unicorn floatie.

Jimmy turned to Delphine with wide, worried eyes.

"Don't worry," Delphine told him, "I'll referee them for you."

Jimmy furrowed his brow and didn't seem entirely convinced but went ahead and cast off from the dock and climbed up into the boat's cockpit.

As the boat glided out of the marina, the passengers' moods lightened. It was a beautiful sunny day; too beautiful to be mad at anyone and almost beautiful enough to forget about a ransomed laptop and a checkered past.

They made their way out into the bay, gliding first one direction then another through the water, which was a million different shades of blue.

Griffin joined Delphine along the railing and gazed at the sparkling surface of the water. "Why is it so many different colors?" she asked.

"Sandbars," said Delphine. "See where the water is lighter? Those are places where it's very shallow, due to a sandbar. It's especially shallow right now, since it's low tide. That's why Jimmy isn't taking the boat in a straight line."

"Ah," said Griffin.

Delphine looked to the back of the boat. Kenji sat on the port side, half-turned on the bench seat to face the water. Marge sat on the starboard side, eyes fixed on the horizon. Their backs were to each other.

"Is something wrong between them?" Griffin asked in a low voice.

"Oh dear," said Delphine. "We need to try to fix this."

"I have an idea," said Griffin. "Follow me."

Delphine was skeptical, but also desperate and tired of trying so hard.

They walked to the back of the boat and stood near the diving platform. Delphine gave Griffin a questioning look, and Griffin returned it with an I've-got-this nod.

"So Delphine," said Griffin.

"Yes dear?" Delphine didn't mind her granddaughter calling her by her first name instead of something like "grandma." The word didn't fit her well, especially since her grandchild was over the age of twelve.

"Have you talked to Kapuni Jones since Fausto's party?"

Marge's head snapped around so fast Delphine felt the breeze. "Is that the nice man who gave us a ride in his bitchin' Mercedes?" she asked.

"Oh yes," said Kenji. "I liked him!"

Delphine's shoulders sagged and Griffin beamed at her.

"Payback, granddaughter of mine," whispered Delphine. Griffin shrugged.

"Well?" asked Marge.

Delphine couldn't form words. She was having quite a time telling lies these days.

"She has!" Marge got up from the bench seat and walked across the deck to sit next to Kenji. "Didn't I tell you, K-Man? The other night at the party, I watched the two of them and didn't I say, 'You just wait, Kenji, Delphine is going to get together with that guy.'"

Kenji nodded. "You did say that."

Marge laughed. "And then you said, you hope she does because she's such a fuddy-duddy and needs to find someone to have fun with."

His eyes darted left and right, as if he knew Delphine was about to come after him and he needed a place to escape to. "Uh, yes."

Griffin said, "He's Miko's uncle."

"Really?" asked Marge. "So if Griffy gets together with Magnum PI and Delphine gets together with Magnum's uncle, you'll both be related in a really super weird way."

"Um," said Griffin.

"And maybe if Delphine has a little fun, she'll leave my boyfriend alone," said Marge.

"You're the one who moved into my room," countered Delphine.

"Oh yeah," said Marge. "Well, still."

Delphine and Griffin sat down on the opposite bench seat and the group fell into silence. The boat's engine purred along as they made their way around one side of the bay. A low wall made of lava rocks came into view. Their formation created a semicircular seawall.

A faint *beep, beep, beep* came from the captain's cockpit above the main cabin.

Griffin pointed at the wall. "What are those rocks?"

"It's an ancient fishpond," said Delphine. The Hawaiians built enclosures so they could raise and feed fish. They practiced very advanced aquaculture techniques."

"Smartypants," mumbled Marge.

More beeping from the cockpit.

"This is supposed to be a nice time," said Delphine in a loud voice. If we can't manage to enjoy each other's company, can we at least remain civil and take advantage of the view and the weather? For heaven's sake." If she wasn't going to get her perfect peaceful solitary vacation, she at least wanted to try for an almost-pleasant boat ride.

"Guys, I hate to disturb your argument, but we have a problem," said Jimmy as he came down the steps from the boat's controls. He lifted one of the bench seats and pulled out five life vests.

CHAPTER 29

The boat tilted forward, and Marge felt her stomach do the same.

"What's going on?" she asked.

"We're taking on water," said Jimmy. He handed Marge a life vest and gave one to Kenji. "Put these on."

Griffin handed one to Delphine, and they all strapped the vests on.

"This is bad," said Marge. Her stomach agreed.

The boat shuddered and made a creaky sound.

"Whoa!" said Griffin, reaching for the railing.

Kenji sprung to his feet. "I have some experience with sinking boats," he announced. "Delphine does too."

"Ha, more like you two have experience with sinking showboats," said Marge. "Look at the two of you, showing off."

"You do not make sense," said Kenji.

"You all need to listen to me carefully," said Jimmy.

Kenji kept talking. "A showboat does not sink."

"Showboat, showoff, This is no time for semiotics," snapped Marge. She wished she'd stayed by the pool instead of going on a dumb boat trip. She could be eating a cheese platter instead of drowning in the bay.

Jimmy said, "I've called the coast guard and they're on the way. Fortunately, I don't think we're sinking too fast—"

"We're *sinking*?" shrieked Marge.

Suddenly the boat lurched under their feet and Marge yelped with fright. She peered over the railing at the water and said, "I think the boat is sitting lower. Oh my goodness, this is it! We're going down!"

A deafening wolf whistle pierced the air, and everyone turned to stare at Griffin. "We need to listen to Jimmy," she said in a calm voice.

"I'll go get the life raft," said Jimmy, enunciating each word. "You all sit tight. Do not try to help, do not jump overboard, and do not freak out. I will be right back." He headed for the bow and disappeared from sight.

"Don't worry, Super Babe, I will save you!" yelled Kenji. He came over to Marge and put his arms around her life vest, and she let him, but only for a second.

She wriggled out of his embrace and put her hands on her hips. "You're impossible. Now help me find a flare gun."

"I believe shooting a flare gun falls into the category of freaking out, which the captain told us not to do," said Delphine.

"He did not say, 'don't look for a flare gun,' did he?" asked Marge.

"Not technically, no," said Griffin, turning

to Delphine for help. Delphine readjusted her life vest.

Jimmy reappeared with a gray cube the size of an ice chest and two lightweight oars. He took everything to the diving platform and pulled a yellow tab sticking out of the side of the cube. A loud *PSSSSSHHHHHHHHHHTTTT* sound emitted from the package as it unfolded and began to take the shape of a four-person life raft.

"I've always wanted to see how those things work," said Marge.

"I am glad this brush with death is helping you cross off your bucket-list item of watching a life raft self-inflate," said Kenji.

Marge glared at him. "Do you really want to go there right now?"

The raft continued to inflate until it took the shape of a fully formed little boat. But the *PSSSSSHHHHHHHHHTTTT* sound didn't stop—the mechanism responsible for shutting off the inflating process must have failed, and ten seconds later, the life raft exploded into thousands of pieces of rubber confetti. Something on the charter boat's dash started beeping again.

"Huh," said Jimmy. "Be right back."

Delphine said, "It's possible we need a new plan." She pointed to a light-blue spot of water not far from the boat. "I think the tide is low enough for us to stand on a sandbar until the Coast Guard gets here."

"I can swim over, but maybe there's an easier way for you to get there." Griffin ran to the side of the boat.

"What does she mean?" Marge asked Delphine. "Is she saying we're too old and feeble to swim to a sandbar?"

Delphine frowned. "Hard to say."

"Child, we will be fine," Marge announced to Griffin, who returned holding the giant unicorn inflatable.

"Ah yes, excellent!" said Kenji when he saw the floatie. He rubbed his hands together. "I will paddle you to safety, Marge."

"Oh brother," said Marge.

Kenji went to work locating the raft oars, which fortunately had not exploded. Next, he inspected the unicorn.

"He's trying to be chivalrous," Delphine whispered to Marge.

"Chauvinistic is more like it," grumbled Marge.

Delphine grabbed onto Marge's life vest and pulled her aside. "Look here. I don't care whether you two stay together or break up or adopt an iguana together. But right now he's trying awfully hard and the least you could do is be civil."

Marge watched as her Kenji Bear ran around the deck wrestling with a giant unicorn floatie, all in the name of wanting to save her. It was pretty sweet, really.

The dying flames of passion flared once again and the temperature in Marge's heart rose a degree or two. "Eh," she said.

"Great. Now let him save you."

To be honest, paddling around on the unicorn floatie sounded fun. "Okay, but you have to come too."

Delphine opened her mouth, but Marge cut her off.

"Do it," Marge commanded.

Surprisingly, Delphine nodded.

Jimmy came back down from the cockpit wearing his own life vest. "I think the boat has stabilized, but just in case, you should all go ahead and get off."

"We'll swim over to that sandbar," said Griffin, pointing to their target destination.

Jimmy noticed Kenji and the unicorn floatie. "Oh man, my niece is gonna kill me."

"We'll buy you a new one," said Delphine in an understanding voice.

"Not necessary," said Jimmy. "But maybe don't leave me a bad Google review."

"Deal," said Delphine.

"Come on, G-ma!" called Griffin. She and Kenji had positioned the inflatable at the back of the boat, on the edge of the diving platform.

"Your unicorn awaits, my lady," Kenji said to Marge as he bowed.

Marge tried not to laugh but failed. "Delphine is coming too."

"That is fine. Let's just get going."

Marge climbed onto the unicorn and motioned for Delphine to get on behind her.

"I'm glad I wore pants," said Delphine.

"Jumpsuits are always the right thing to wear," said Marge with pride.

Kenji carefully fit himself on the unicorn in front of Marge, and Griffin handed him an oar.

"Ready?" asked Griffin.

"You betcha," said Marge. "Griffy, give the horse's butt a shove!"

CHAPTER 30

The Coast Guard picked up Griffin, Kenji, Marge, and Delphine from the sandbar and took them back to the marina. The ride back in from the bay went quickly, but Delphine had plenty of time to think about the events of the day so far. Unfortunately, not a lot of it fit together very well, like someone had put the contents of two jigsaw puzzles into one box. But by the time Miko met them at the dock, she had a vague idea of what to do next.

"Everyone okay?" asked Miko. He looked at Griffin a little longer than everyone else.

"Yeah, we're fine," said Griffin. "Just a little wet." She wrung out the hem of her shirt.

"Have you heard anything about Jimmy's boat?" asked Delphine.

The Coast Guard officer who helped them disembark joined the conversation. "Our captain let us know the boat is fine. They're towing it in to get inspected but they don't think it's anything real serious."

Delphine wasn't so sure, but an inspection would reveal the truth.

"Thanks for the update," said Miko. "That boat is Jimmy's livelihood. He has insurance but it would've been bad if it sank."

"I wonder what caused the problem," said Delphine.

"Good question," said Miko. "I guess it's always possible he could've run into a sandbar or a reef, but he knows the bay pretty well."

"I'm sure his insurance company will do a full investigation," said the Coast Guard officer.

Delphine looked and Kenji and based on his expression, she knew he was thinking the same thing she was.

They said their goodbyes to the Coast Guard crew and walked along the docks.

"What an adventure!" said Marge. "Made me kind of hungry though. Let's go back to the resort for a snack."

"Good idea," said Kenji.

"Actually, we have another stop to make first," said Delphine. Kenji gave her his what-have-you-got-in-mind? expression. "Miko, does your uncle live nearby?"

"Super close," said Miko.

Delphine put her hand to her hair, as if making it presentable would be possible after they'd paddled around on a unicorn inflatable and got rescued from a sandbar. "I'd like to pay him a visit."

"What do you have up your sleeve, Delphine?" asked Kenji.

"Kapuni Jones might be able to shed some light on who just tried to kill us," said Delphine.

"You're not implying my uncle had anything to do with it," said Miko, sounding defensive.

"I certainly hope not. But we need to talk to him. Can you take us please?"

Miko looked uncertain. "I'm not sure I like this, but if it helps get to the bottom of everything, let's go. I'll text him to let him know we're coming."

"But I wanted a snack!" said Marge.

"Why don't you and Griffin go back to the resort?" said Delphine. She hoped with all her might Marge would take her suggestion.

"No way. If you and Kenji are going, I'm going." Marge put her hands on her hips.

"We'll all go," said Griffin, turning to Delphine for confirmation. Delphine nodded.

Miko put his phone away. "He says to come on over."

Instead of walking to the parking lot like Delphine expected, they made a left turn and walked down another maze of docks. This raised a lot of questions, but Delphine hoped they'd get a whole lot of answers very soon.

"How did you hear about what happened to Jimmy's boat?" Delphine asked Miko, trying to switch gears.

"I texted him," said Griffin. "I kind of panicked, I guess."

Miko smiled at her. "I'm glad you texted."

Delphine's romance radar pinged. For Griffin's sake, she hoped Miko's uncle was above board.

"But if I had known we were socializing after our shipwreck, I would've asked you to bring me some dry clothes," she said to him.

"Sorry," said Delphine. "But there's no time to waste." She too wished they could've had time to freshen up a little. Her linen pants had gotten soaked up to her knees. They were almost dry now but still damp enough to appear as if she wore two-tone trousers. But she was on her way to perform an interrogation, and that took precedence over tidying up.

"These are super nice boats," said Griffin as they strolled by a sixty-foot yacht.

"We just passed one with a hot tub on it," said Marge.

"Oh, a hot tub sounds nice," said Griffin.

"If you want, you can use Fausto's Jacuzzi," Miko told her. "The pool too."

"Really?" asked Griffin.

"Yeah. He left yesterday to start pre-production on his next movie, and none of the family is due to visit for the rest of the month."

Delphine was disappointed to learn Fausto had left the island;

she would've liked to have said goodbye to him. But maybe she'd be back again soon. Yes, maybe she could find some way to sneak over for a vacation all by herself. She wouldn't make the mistake of bringing Marge and Kenji along next time.

"That all sounds super relaxing," said Griffin. "Thanks." She smiled and put a hand on Miko's arm, then quickly removed it, as if embarrassed by the display of affection.

Kenji, who had been walking right next to Delphine, elbowed her in the ribs and raised his eyebrows.

Delphine nodded and put a finger to her lips, begging him to let it be for now. Marge was busy ogling another superyacht and didn't notice the exchange. Thank goodness.

They approached the end of a long stretch of dock. In the very last slip bobbed a tiny, rusty metal dinghy. Kapuni Jones sat on the splintered wooden seat, holding a fishing rod that appeared to be older than the boat. The vessel could only be called tiny and floated lower in the water than all the other boats. Everyone had to peer down at him from the dock.

"You expect us to go down there, after what we just went through?" Marge stage-whispered to Delphine.

"Ah, guests!" said Kapuni. He put down his fishing rod.

He wore his Dodgers bucket hat and usual outfit of black T-shirt and chino shorts. Delphine thought he looked quite fetching, really, as she got more used to seeing him. She stopped in her tracks. Were sharks cute?

"Hello, Uncle," said Miko. "You remember everyone from the other night—this is Kenji and his girlfriend, Marge."

"Right now I'm more like his good friend," said Marge.

Kenji let out a hoarse whimper. Kapuni waved hello at them.

"And Griffin," Miko said, pointing to her.

"Ah yes, the lovely granddaughter of the even lovelier Delphine," said Kapuni. He saluted Griffin with two fingers to his bucket hat, but his eyes remained glued to Delphine.

Delphine blushed and hoped no one noticed her embarrassment.

"She's my granddaughter too," said Marge. "And I am also lovely."

"Naturally," said Kapuni. "You are all lovely."

"Can we get down to business?" said Kenji.

"Oh, business, eh?" said Kapuni. "Okay, well I suppose—"

Before Kapuni could continue, Kenji walked over to the ladder next to the boat and prepared to climb down to sit in the dinghy with their host.

"Oh, no, not in this shit bucket," said Kapuni, putting out a hand out to prevent Kenji from advancing.

"Your boat's not *that* bad," said Griffin. "I mean, it's not great but it's not a sh—"

Kapuni cut her off. "No, no, it's the name of my boat."

"The name of your boat is the…" Griffin hesitated.

"The *Shit Bucket*," said Kapuni. "Perfect name, right? I mean, just look at it!"

Delphine covered her mouth but couldn't hold back a laugh. It really was the perfect name for the junky little boat.

Kapuni stood up in the dinghy and picked up a plastic five-gallon bucket sitting near his feet. "Take this, Nephew," he said, and handed it up to Miko.

"That's not a bucket full of … of … poop, is it?" asked Marge, wrinkling her nose. "Like a literal bucket of sh—"

"Do you think I'm some kind of weirdo?" said Kapuni. "I went fishing. This is dinner."

Sounds of relief came from more than one person in the group.

Delphine watched Kapuni climb out of the boat. He did a little jump as he came off the last ladder rung and stuck the landing, his bare feet making a dull thud on the dock. He smiled at her with a twinkle in his eye.

"Let us go enjoy the fancy feast," he said. He beckoned to his guests and started off down the dock.

"Does he mean enjoy *a* fancy feast?" stage-whispered Marge.

"Yes, but he also means the *Fancy Feast*," said Kapuni.

"I don't get it," said Marge.

They came to a sudden stop one slip down from the dinghy and almost ran into each other; no one had expected to walk such a short distance. In front of them floated a boat dripping with so much luxury it made Marge gasp.

"Holy smokes," she said.

The vessel was all sleek lines and tinted windows. The chrome railings along the decks shone in the afternoon sun and those surfaces not made of gleaming metal were the cleanest, shiniest white Delphine had ever seen—and she'd seen plenty of yachts in her day.

Above the cabin towered the bridge, complete with high-tech radar and communication antennae affixed to the roof. It would be easy to communicate with Norway using all that equipment, thought Delphine.

"Wow," said Kenji.

"I'll say," said Delphine.

She really hoped Kapuni Jones was part of their solution, and not part of their problem.

CHAPTER 31

A young woman with long, jet-black hair appeared on the deck of Kapuni's boat. Momi. Today instead of a black suit, she wore a dark-blue bikini top with white plumeria flowers printed on it and a matching sarong. She waved at them but did not smile.

Kapuni boarded and also waved to them. "Welcome aboard the *Fancy Feast*." He pointed to the back of the boat, which faced them, and sure enough, the unusual name had been painted in ornate script along the stern.

Miko got on first, followed by Griffin, Marge, Kenji, and finally Delphine. Kapuni held his arm out for her to take as she came across the gangplank.

"Thank you," she said.

Kapuni cleared his throat. "Everyone, you remember Momi, my niece. Miko's cousin."

Momi gave them a tiny bow.

"Hi Mommy!" said Marge.

Delphine cringed. "Dear, I think it's—"

Kapuni put a hand on Delphine's arm. "It's okay, she's used to it. Happens more than you'd think. Now come with me, everyone." Kapuni led the way into the cabin.

Delphine stopped in front of Momi. "Do you also captain the yacht?"

Momi nodded. Delphine wondered if Momi drove the boat like she drove Kapuni's Mercedes, but she wasn't sure she wanted to find out.

Kapuni escorted them through the cabin to the front of the yacht, which featured a view of all the boats entering and leaving the marina. A table had been set for six, complete with sterling silver flatware, linen napkins, and fine crystal glassware. Everything had been arranged so no one would have to sit with their back to the bay; they'd all have a fine view.

"Have a seat," said Kapuni. He sat down, and Delphine didn't hesitate to take the chair next to him.

Miko and Griffin took seats next to each other, as did Kenji and Marge.

"Thank you for having us over, Uncle," said Miko.

"No biggie, Nephew," said Kapuni.

"What a beautiful view," said Delphine.

"So tell me, Mr. Jones," said Kenji, and Delphine readied herself to get into the subject they'd come to discuss.

"Yes?" said Kapuni.

"What inspired you to name your superyacht after a cat food?"

Kapuni looked at Miko. "What is he talking about?"

"I'll tell you later," Miko said.

They all gazed out at the beautiful blue water. The boat rocked just enough to be noticeable but not threatening (considering the earlier mishap), and tiny waves lapped at the hull, creating a relaxing, pleasant sound. It was an environment Delphine could easily get used to.

"This boat's not gonna sink, is it?" asked Marge.

Kapuni laughed heartily. "Not if I can help it!"

Marge leaned over to Delphine and said, "He doesn't exactly make you feel confident about the situation, does he."

Delphine coughed.

"Delphine, why are we here exactly?" asked Griffin.

"I am still not sure about that either, to be honest," said Kenji.

Kapuni held up his hand. "No shop talk until we have eaten. You all need sustenance after your harrowing experience."

"Ain't it the truth!" said Marge as she patted her stomach.

"You are in luck. Momi has prepared a gourmet treat for us this afternoon."

Marge clapped always excited when it came to food. "Yay!"

"I don't understand how you could prepare a gourmet meal if you didn't know we were coming until a few minutes ago," said Griffin.

Kapuni put a finger to the side of his nose. "Momi is a genius in the kitchen. You'll see."

Momi appeared at the table with a silver tray carrying a plastic liter bottle of store-brand apple juice and six ice-filled juice glasses.

"Ah, the first course!" Kapuni unfolded his napkin onto his lap as Momi poured.

Momi came back a minute later with a huge silver bowl overflowing with Lay's Classic potato chips and placed it on the table. Everyone dug in. Next, each of them received a cut-crystal bowl filled with fruit cocktail, right out of the can, complete with heavy syrup.

"So exciting," said Kapuni. "Now comes the main course."

"This is very fancy," said Kenji.

"Yes," said Kapuni. "I enjoy the finer things in life."

"I've always thought of fruit cocktail as a delicacy," said Marge.

Delphine couldn't figure out if everyone was trying to be funny or not. It was either that, or they were starstruck from the luxury of the boat. In any case, she wasn't a fan of the fruit cocktail.

Momi reappeared again, carrying a large platter of sandwich halves, which she set in the center of the table. Tuna fish sandwiches, on white bread.

Kapuni spread his arms wide. "Dig in!"

Kenji was the first to dig. He took two halves and put them on his plate. Griffin followed, then Miko. Delphine took one half and so did Kapuni.

"Isn't most of this food processed?" Delphine asked Kapuni.

"It's cheat day," said Kapuni.

Delphine wondered if every day was cheat day for Kapuni Jones.

After eating a bite of her sandwich, she discovered the bread was artisanal sourdough; fragrant and zingy. The sandwich was anything but ordinary. Flavorful fish and delicate spices exploded on her tongue. Next-level tuna salad.

She put a few chips on her plate, as well as another sandwich half. The combination was too good to pass up, despite being almost full.

Everyone at the table, focused on their food. The only sounds were potato-chip crunching and the faint creaking of the ropes mooring the boat. For a moment everyone seemed to have forgotten why they'd come.

"These are the best tuna sandwiches I have ever had in my life," said Kenji. "They are as luxurious as your boat."

Kapuni beamed with pride. "Nothing but the best for my special guests."

"I like this guy," Marge said to Delphine. "You two are friends, huh?"

"Oh, I don't know. Friends is such a relative term..." said Delphine.

"We are friends, yes," said Kapuni.

Delphine put down her half-eaten half sandwich. "Mr. Jones, I have some questions for you about what happened to us earlier today."

Kapuni, whose plate and fruit bowl were empty, dabbed at his lips with his napkin and scrutinized her. "I'm all ears."

"We went out on Jimmy DuPree's boat this morning," said

Delphine. "Once we got out into the bay, it took on water and almost sank. Everything ended up being fine, but—"

"Thank goodness!" said Kapuni. "I like Jimmy. It would be a real shame if he lost his boat."

"And we are all fine, thank you for asking," said Delphine.

"Yes, you look terrific," he said.

Delphine forged ahead. "Were you responsible for trying to sink Jimmy's boat?"

Kapuni pointed to his chest. "Me?"

"Yes, you. You and the two people I saw you talking to at the hotel pool yesterday afternoon."

Momi came back out onto the deck and put another silver tray on the table. This one was stacked high with Nutter Butter cookies.

Kenji reached for a cookie. "Delphine, are you saying he is involved with the theft and ransoming of my laptop? In which case, what the heck, Mr. Jones?"

"Delphine, let me get this straight. You are wondering if I stole your friend's laptop and tried to sink Jimmy's boat?" Kapuni asked.

"Correct. And I want to know if you're in on it with the Norwegians."

"So … three things," said Kapuni.

"Yes." Delphine eyed the cookies.

"And also you think I'm ransoming Mr. Yamamoto's laptop, so now that's four things you want to know."

"Do you honestly think my uncle would try to sink my best friend's boat?" Miko asked. "And steal a laptop?"

Griffin put a hand on his arm. "Maybe she has a good reason to ask."

"There better be a really good reason," said Miko. "Because you're making a hefty accusation."

Marge sat and watched the action, quiet for once. She popped cookies into her mouth like she was munching on popcorn at the movies.

Kapuni finished a cookie. "You have a very long list."

"You don't seem surprised I'm suggesting you might have tried to kill us," said Delphine, giving him a piercing glare. His eyes were clear, free of malice. A good sign, but she still couldn't be sure.

"When you get to be my age and have seen as much I have, nothing is surprising anymore," said Kapuni. "Except when I met you. So charming and coy—you really threw me for a loop." He wiggled his eyebrows at her and one side of her mouth rose in a smile.

"And besides," he continued. "Why would I try to kill you when I'm trying to get you to go on a date?"

"He asked you out?" said Griffin, Miko, Marge, and Kenji all at the same time.

"Maybe you're mad because I said no," countered Delphine.

"Oh gosh. I like you a lot, but my ego isn't that fragile." Kapuni laughed so hard his Dodgers hat almost fell off.

Delphine's lips pressed into an angry straight line.

"As for the laptop," said Kapuni, "as you can see, I am not without means. I don't need to steal electronic equipment."

Delphine wanted to point out it was less about the electronic equipment and more about the software on it. But mentioning this fact would give away too much.

"What about the people you were talking to at the pool yesterday?" asked Delphine, circling back around to the next item on her list.

Kapuni gasped. "Was that you hiding behind those ferns?"

Delphine glared at him but said nothing. Marge chortled.

He shrugged. "Those two? I'd just met them in the pool. We got to talking."

"I heard you mention pineapples," said Delphine. In her mind it seemed like this point could be important or relevant somehow, but now it sounded kind of silly.

"I often talk about pineapples," said Kapuni. "I like pineapples. And I like giving people tips for where to find good pineapples, which is what I was doing for them, if you must know."

He still sounded pleasant, but a hint of frustration had crept into his tone. She decided to put the pressure on. But before she could, Kenji joined in.

"It all seems plausible," said Kenji.

"That Mr. Jones is a thief?" asked Griffin.

"No, that he is connected to the ransomers. But Delphine, if he is a thief, you are friends with a criminal," Kenji said.

"My uncle isn't a criminal!" said Miko.

"Can you really be sure, dear?" Delphine asked Miko. "No offense," she said to Kapuni.

Kapuni grinned. "None taken. Besides, it takes one to know one, as they say."

Griffin laughed.

To hide her consternation, Delphine picked up her glass of apple juice and took a drink. She desperately wished for water instead, but it felt like the wrong time to ask.

"In any case, I have a feeling you're well acquainted with the art of thievery," she said.

In truth, Delphine wasn't sure what they were implying or not implying at his point in the conversation. She'd confused even herself. She felt like Kapuni's boat was starting to sink like Jimmy's had. But it was only her imagination—the sensation of drowning in this conversation, where things weren't going as well as she'd hoped. Then again, what should she have expected after accusing their host of attempted murder?

"I didn't try to kill anyone," Kapuni said to her. "And I didn't steal a laptop. But I will help you get it back if you agree to go on a date with me."

"Fine," said Delphine.

CHAPTER 32

Kapuni's guests polished off the last of the Nutter Butters, and Miko drove Marge, Delphine, and Kenji from the marina to the hotel in one of the resort's shuttle vans. Kenji made a point to sit next to Marge in the back seat and worked up his courage to talk to her once Miko got on the road.

"I am sorry about the boat ride," he said.

"It wasn't your fault," said Marge, yawning. "In fact, you saved my life with a daring rescue on a unicorn floatie."

She'd exaggerated, but he would take the compliment. He smiled at her and reached for her hand, and she let him hold it. His stomach felt all nice and warm again. A pleasant change after being frozen out for a day.

"I promise we will get this stupid laptop thing figured out, and then I will spend the rest of the vacation making it up to you," Kenji told her.

"Oh yeah? How are you gonna do that?" asked Marge.

"You will just have to wait and see," said Kenji. "But first we have some things to take care of."

"Don't worry, Kenji Bear, we'll get your computer back. And I'll help however I can. Even if it means staying out of your hair." She reached out and messed up his already messed-up hair.

They both laughed.

The van pulled into the resort's circular drive and Miko turned off the engine. He informed Delphine that earlier in the morning, he'd gotten the room number for Minka and Martin Solberg. The siblings were sharing a two-room luxury bungalow, of which there were only three in the entire resort.

"How about photos?" asked Kenji.

"Still working on those. I'll text them to you as soon as I can," said Miko.

This was good, thought Kenji. A room number was progress. And hopefully soon they would know what their persons of interest looked like.

Delphine sighed. "I think we should pay them a visit this evening, once it's dark."

She'd read his mind, as she often did. Kenji checked his watch. "We have a little time to strategize."

"And have dinner," added Marge. Kenji loved how she always approached things from her stomach's point of view. Getting plenty of sustenance was always important.

They decided to meet in Delphine's room in two hours to put a plan together. Kenji went back to his room for a shower. Delphine and Marge headed back to the suite to freshen up as well. Griffin and Miko went to the club's restaurant to check in with Davis and try to get photos of the Solbergs.

Kenji lay on his bed, wishing Marge were there. Not so they could indulge in any funny business, but so he could hear her laugh, and see her smile. He wanted to be around her all the time, really. But first, several things had to occur. He'd have to get his damn laptop back and second, he'd have to prove to Marge she was the most important thing in his life. Not work, not Delphine —Marge.

After taking a long hot shower, Kenji tried to take a nap but soon gave up and wandered over to Delphine's suite. She let him in and invited him to sit out on the giant balcony with her and Marge.

"Fancy setup," said Kenji, looking around the interior as they walked through the main room.

"Yes, and far too big for just one person, apparently," said Delphine.

"Really?" asked Marge.

"She was being sarcastic," Kenji told Marge.

Marge shook her head. "And thank you for mansplaining."

"You are welcome," said Kenji.

"She was being sarcastic," Delphine told Kenji.

"Oh. Sorry," he said sheepishly.

A knock sounded on the door and Delphine went to answer it.

"I ordered some room service for everyone, so we can have snacks before we ... whatever it is we are doing," Marge told Kenji.

"I do not think you should be involved with our plan," Kenji said as Delphine returned with Griffin and Miko in tow.

"What, you don't think I can handle myself?" Marge's tone implied she was on her way to the danger zone and Kenji recoiled. Good thing food was imminent; eating always seemed to make her feel better.

"I think you should let her come along," said Delphine. Marge puffed up her chest and appeared vindicated.

Kenji's jaw dropped. "What?"

"Sure, why not? This could be dangerous, or worse. Let her see what we're dealing with, what we used to deal with," said Delphine.

"What exactly did you used to deal with?" asked Griffin. She and Miko sat down on the couch opposite Kenji and Marge, and Delphine sat next to Griffin.

"Yeah." Marge sounded like she really wanted to know, but she looked a little worried, as if afraid to hear the answer.

Kenji realized what Delphine had done. She'd set up a chance for them to tell the important people in their lives what they used to do. For decades, they'd kept it all to themselves, always blowing off questions about their professions with vague answers and never letting anyone get too close. But they could both change all of that right now.

They had nothing to lose. Or, they had everything to lose, depending on how he looked at it. Would it be better to be honest with Marge, or to protect her from his past? And how sneaky of Delphine to make it seem like it was all his choice to spill the beans.

Everyone was waiting for him to say something. He glanced at Delphine. They nodded at each other.

"We used to be spies," he said.

"Ohhhhhh," said Griffin, letting the words sink in. "That does kind of explain a lot."

"Yes," said Kenji. "For an agency called—"

Delphine raised a hand and interrupted him. "I don't think we need to bore them with all the tiny details."

Kenji said, "Right. Of course. Well, we used to be top-secret spies for an international agency. It was dangerous. We have seen things most people have not. And maybe we have done some not-so-nice things."

"Huh," said Miko. He leaned back on the couch. "What an interesting group of people. We've got ex-CIA, ex-FBI, and ex-whatever-you-guys-were."

"We could form a badass detective agency!" suggested Griffin.

"Hey," that would be fun," said Marge. "We could catch all sorts of bad guys. Or, you know, we could form a cool criminal gang!"

Kenji remembered Marge's story about getting mixed up with a group of jewel thieves before she came to Los Angeles. But she sworn she was innocent, and didn't want to have anything to do with people like that anymore. And he believed her. So he laughed at her joke. But no one else laughed.

"I mean, the law is kind of a grey area anyway, right?" asked Marge.

Delphine scowled. "Not really."

"Nope," said Griffin.

Kenji wanted to get back to the subject at hand. "We can decide what kind of gang to form later. But right now … Marge, now I have told you what I used to do. Are we okay?"

Marge picked up a bunch of grapes from a platter on the coffee table and plucked them all off the vine. "It's a lot to process," she said. She placed the handful of grapes on the table. One of them rolled off the table, across the balcony, and disappeared over the edge.

Kenji felt and heard anxiety hit his digestive system—*gurgle, glurp*!

Marge stood up and began pacing. "Okay, so … you two used to be super-secret spies. And Kenji, you're still doing consulting. So you're kind of still a spy. And your laptop must have had some top-secret stuff on it. Someone stole it, and you need to get it back … and all it sounds real dangerous."

"It is dangerous, yes," said Kenji.

"You think the thieves are connected to your past somehow," said Griffin.

"Correct," said Kenji. "Marge, are you mad at me for keeping this from you?"

Marge stopped pacing. She frowned as she took a deep breath in and let it out in one big huff. Kenji had never been so scared in his life, and that was saying something.

"Actually," she said, "My boyfriend is a badass spy and I think it's terrific!" She clapped her hands and did a little jump.

Kenji almost melted with relief. He pulled Marge down to sit next to him and gave her a kiss on the cheek; he didn't care who saw.

Griffin put a hand on Delphine's arm. "Thanks for finally telling me. It's been driving me nuts for years!"

Delphine smiled. "Just don't tell anyone I told you."

"You don't want to blow your cover," said Griffin.

"Kind of," said Delphine. "I also don't want to blow anyone else's cover. In our family, I mean."

Griffin's eyes went wide. "Do you mean…?"

"Yes, you could consider this the family business. But keep it under your hat for now." Delphine raised an eyebrow at her granddaughter.

"Right. So how can Miko and I help?" asked Griffin, leaning forward.

"You can help by leaving," said Delphine.

"That seems too easy," said Miko. "And kind of boring."

"What's boring?" asked Griffin, pretending to have forgotten the discussion.

"I think what she means is you two should not be involved," said Kenji.

"I think they got it, K-Man," said Marge. "Sarcasm?"

"Oh," said Kenji. He felt too stressed out to keep up with the jokes.

Miko stood up. "In that case, Griffin, how about we go get some dinner?"

Griffin's stomach growled. "Perfect. Delphine, thanks for telling us about your, uh, employment history. Your secret is safe with us, right?" She looked to Miko and then to Marge.

"You betcha," said Marge, and Miko nodded.

They said their goodbyes, and Delphine, Marge, and Kenji sat on the balcony watching darkness descend on the bay.

"I think it might rain," said Delphine.

"Maybe so," said Kenji, deep in thought.

"So, what's the plan?" asked Marge as she rubbed her palms together. "This is gonna be fun."

CHAPTER 33

A light rain fell as Delphine, Kenji, and Marge began their walk to the far end of the resort, where Minka and Martin Solberg had rented a private bungalow for the week. Fortunately it wasn't pouring, but it came down hard enough to leave Delphine wishing she had an umbrella. But who brings an umbrella on a tropical vacation?

Delphine had changed into her most comfortable blazer and linen pants for the night's events, and Marge wore a navy-blue pantsuit, saying the dark fabric made her feel like a cat burglar. The looks Kenji gave her at the mention of "cat burglar" had made Delphine want to leave the room. Kenji had on what he usually wore: shorts and an MIT T-shirt.

The three had spent an hour eating appetizers and going over a loosely defined "plan" of action. There were too many variables to create a true plan, but Delphine didn't see this as a problem. In their line of work, they always had to keep things fluid.

Delphine had used at least twenty-five of their sixty-minute prep session making Marge promise she would stay back and let Kenji do the talking. Marge said she'd abide, but added if something went wrong, she wouldn't hesitate to come to her Kenji

Bear's rescue. It was anyone's guess as to how things might play out.

"Hold up," said Kenji, and he stopped under a large koa tree. They were close to bungalows now, standing in front of what appeared to be the last building containing multiple hotel rooms. The stone path had turned into a gravel walkway, and it was darker in this area—instead of lamp posts lighting the way, only a series of twelve-inch-tall walkway lights lined the path. Everyone's knees looked great in the glow.

The rain dripped through the leaves of the koa tree and landed on Delphine in large heavy drops. "What is it?" she asked Kenji.

"Coo! Coo!" Kenji sang out.

"Coo!" sang someone in the bushes to their left.

Out stepped Kapuni Jones wearing a rain parka and carrying his backpack. "You guys are under-dressed."

If Delphine hadn't been soaked, she might've been less crabby. "Really."

Kapuni unzipped his backpack and pulled out three ultra-thin rain parkas, the kind found in the impulse purchase section of a drugstore.

"This would have been nice ten minutes ago," said Marge, but she took one and unfolded it from its little pouch and put it on.

"You're welcome," said Kapuni.

Kenji and Delphine put theirs on too.

"What are you doing here?" asked Delphine.

"Kenji asked me to come. I said I'd help, remember? So here I am."

Delphine wished Kenji would have told her he'd invited an unwanted guest. "But you weren't there for our planning session. You don't know what's going on."

"Eh," said Kapuni. "You can't really plan for these things. Besides, I brought this. I'd say it's a good plan." He removed a small pistol from his backpack.

"You can't come, and you definitely can't bring that thing," hissed Delphine.

"Which is it? I can't come, or I can only come if I don't bring Lucinda?" asked Kapuni.

"You named your gun?" asked Marge.

Kapuni Jones nodded.

"Cool." Marge sounded a little awestruck.

"I named my gun too," said Kenji.

"Oh yeah? What do you call it?" asked Marge.

"Umm," said Kenji.

"Wait, is naming your gun a euphemism?" asked Marge. "Or is that a euphonium…"

"No, that's like a tuba," said Kapuni.

Delphine felt a tension headache coming on. "Kenji, name your weapon later. Marge, stop talking. Kapuni, put your gun away. Someone might see it."

Kapuni leaned over to Marge. "Is she always this bossy?"

"Uh-huh," said Marge and Kenji.

Kapuni bobbed his head and grinned at Delphine. "I like it."

"I'm not in charge," said Delphine. "Kenji is in charge. But can we just go?"

"Right," said Kenji. "Marge, you stay about twenty feet back from the door, to the left. I will knock. Delphine, you take the right side, Kapuni, the left."

"I think Kapuni should stay with Marge," said Delphine.

"Okay but he has the gun," explained Kenji.

Kapuni held up the pistol. "And I will not let you—"

Delphine snatched the weapon out of his hand and put it in her pocket. "Kapuni, you are with Marge. Kenji, you knock, and I'll go to whatever side doesn't put me in front of a window. Let's go."

They moved out and silently made their way to bungalow 2. Delphine stayed to the right, away from the window to the left of the door. Kapuni and Marge stopped behind a nearby palm tree so thin, it did nothing to actually hide them.

Kenji went up to the door and knocked.

No one answered.

He knocked again and waited.

"I guess they are out," he said, scratching the back of his head.

"Did we make a plan for what to do if no one was home?" whispered Marge from behind the tree.

"No," said Kenji. "Ding-dang, I am losing my touch."

"Well I'm not losing mine," said Delphine. She performed the traditional check-left-then-right move to make sure the coast was clear, got out her universal key card from the blazer pocket not weighed down by Lucinda, and was about to place the card on the card pad when the door opened. She slid the key card into the sleeve of her blazer.

A giant Samoan man stood in the open doorway, filling it from top to bottom and side to side. "What's up? You got our food?"

Miko hadn't been able to get them photos of Minka and Martin yet, but Delphine could say with reasonable certainty the person in front of them was not a member of the Solberg family.

"Um, is Martin here?" asked Kenji, sounding like he wanted to see if his friend could come out to play.

"No brah, do you see him? I don't see him." The giant's eyes flicked from side to side.

"Who's at the door?" yelled a man from inside the bungalow. Delphine couldn't see anyone, but the voice sounded like it belonged to someone as big as the person in front of them. "They got food?"

"Nah," said the boulder at the door.

"Do you know when Martin will be back?" asked Kenji.

The huge man laughed. "Brah, do I look like his mommy? How would I know? He's not here. Now unless you got seven double orders of hot wings for me and my bruddah, I think you better go."

Delphine tugged at Kenji's rain parka, and they walked away as the giant slammed the door.

The four seniors crept slowly back the way they'd come. After a minute, Kenji stopped and Marge, Delphine, and Kapuni gathered around him. It was quiet except for the sound of big drops of water hitting their cheap rain parkas.

"I am very confused," said Kenji. "Did we go to the wrong room?"

"No, Miko said bungalow two," said Delphine.

"I wonder if we should go back," said Delphine. "Maybe we need to try to talk to that man."

"I suppose we should," agreed Kenji.

Delphine tried not to yawn but failed. Then Kenji and Marge yawned too. She felt too old to be solving crime after dark. "Okay. Let's think this through."

"Wait a second," said Kapuni.

"What?" asked Marge.

Kapuni shifted his weight from foot to foot. "I recognized that guy."

"From where?" asked Kenji.

"I can't say."

"Can't rat on a business associate?" asked Delphine.

"No," he said as his eyes met hers.

"Do you mean, 'No, I cannot rat on an associate,' or, 'No, you are wrong?'" asked Kenji.

Kapuni kept his mouth shut.

"Let me guess," said Marge. "You know him from church."

"Yes, church," said Kapuni. "He is a god-fearing man. But maybe better left alone."

"Is he an enforcer?" Delphine asked him.

"No, a farmer."

"I am still very confused," said Kenji. "And very, very screwed."

"Now K-Man, don't worry." Marge adjusted the hood of her parka. "All's not lost yet."

"It sure feels like all is lost," said Kenji.

"Let's leave them alone for now," said Kapuni. He looked at Delphine and his expression asked her to please take his advice.

Delphine gazed down and discovered she stood in a big

puddle. That seemed about right. Everywhere she went she ended up in puddles. And now she was so tired she was assigning life metaphors to rainy sidewalks. Suddenly she couldn't wait to get back to her room and take a bath and pretend all this wasn't happening. She needed time to think. "Let's go," she said. They began walking again.

The man in the bungalow had to know Minka and Martin, since the reservation was in their names. Perhaps the Norwegians were in Hawaii on some sort of business trip. She'd originally thought running into them had been total coincidence; they'd come to the island for vacation just like she, Kenji, and Marge had. And maybe it still was coincidence, but maybe they were up to something besides relaxation.

In any event, Kapuni knew the giant Samoan in the bungalow, but was playing coy. Why?

Delphine fell into step next to Kapuni. "Why can't you tell us who those men are and how you know them?"

"Frustrating, isn't it," said Kapuni, shaking his head.

"More like suspicious."

"Yeah, I could see that."

"You must cross some very interesting lines on a regular basis."

"You have no idea," he said.

Had he suggested they leave those men in bungalow 2 alone for her and Kenji's best interest, or for his own best interest? Withholding information made Kapuni Jones seem like he was up to something, yet he tried to act light and breezy, as if he had nothing to hide. Perhaps he suffered from some kind of antisocial personality disorder.

In any case, he was about to drive her crazy.

Delphine felt resentful about… Well, she didn't know what she resented at this point, but she was cranky at having to play games while soaking wet and cold. And it was past her bedtime.

They'd almost made it back to Delphine's room, and she grew madder every second Kapuni stayed silent.

He put a hand on her arm and stopped her on the path. The rain still tap-tapped on their parkas and Delphine scowled at him.

"Look," he said. "I want to help you. More than you know. But I live on this island. You and your friends will leave at the end of your vacation, but I have to stay. I need to give this some thought and make sure I protect everyone involved the best I can. Especially you."

His gray eyes met hers and his gaze was so earnest Delphine wanted to believe him. There were so many reasons not to though.

CHAPTER 34

After the previous night's fails, Delphine had suggested they all meet on the beach for breakfast the following morning and figure out what to do next. This was the big day, after all—the day Kenji was supposed to meet the ransomers. And they still didn't have a plan.

As they ate, Kenji filled Griffin and Miko in on what had happened at the bungalow. Which didn't take long.

"Well, I have all kinds of information for you," said Miko. He handed over a photo of the Solberg siblings—a grainy black and white image of them standing at the check-in counter. It was hard to see details, but easy to tell they looked like their parents, Olafur and Lilja. Same facial structures and hair coloring.

"What else you got for us, Magnum?" said Marge. She was clearly enjoying playing detective, although she sounded more like a TV detective than an educated operative.

"I heard from Jimmy about his boat," said Miko

"Oh," said Delphine, leaning forward in her chair.

"Yeah. The cause of the leak wasn't sabotage."

"What was it?" asked Kenji.

"They said it was some kind of plastic seal that had deteriorated. Like around the engine? I don't know, I'm not very mechanically inclined," admitted Miko. "But apparently last time Jimmy took his boat in for maintenance, the guy didn't catch the problem. It was never a very big leak, but Jimmy had no way of knowing at the time."

Kenji frowned. "Well that is disappointing."

"Oh yeah," said Marge. "Real disappointing no one tried to kill us yesterday. Honestly, you people need to reexamine your priorities."

"You're right," said Delphine.

Marge's face scrunched up with confusion. "I am?"

Griffin and Miko excused themselves to take care of an errand for the Conte estate—something about a delivery of Italian antiques being delivered. Kenji left to go lie down in his room; his stomach was acting up. He'd told them he might have eaten something bad, but Delphine knew it was stress. Unfortunately, there wasn't much she could do to help him feel better. Neither of them had come up with any ideas, and time was running out.

According to the original ransom text, Kenji was supposed to meet with the ransomers, AKA Minka and Martin, that afternoon, although they still didn't know where or exactly what time.

Delphine stayed on the beach because she wanted some outdoor time to collect her thoughts, and apparently Marge wanted to bother Delphine, because she'd refused to go away. They'd set up in a spot under some palm trees. It was only nine, but the sky was cloudless and already she knew the day would be a warm one.

Delphine opened one eye to watch Marge as she tried for what must've been the millionth time to get comfortable in her lounge chair. She flopped over from her stomach to lie on her back, straight as a board.

"Are you sure it's safe for us to be out here?" asked Marge.

"Why, is it making you nervous?"

"You bet your bippie it's making me nervous," said Marge. She got up and adjusted the chair so she could sit upright and look out at the water.

"You can always go back to the room," Delphine reminded her.

"No," said Marge.

Delphine put her chair into a seated position too. She slipped on her sunglasses and admired the blue-green bay. She'd been to many beaches in many countries, but something about this place had captured her heart, even with all the unwanted drama of the past three days. She vowed once again to come back sometime on her own. If it were actually possible to detach herself from Marge.

"I suppose it's a little risky to stay out here," said Delphine. "But there are quite a few people around this morning, and I doubt Minka and Martin would try anything out in the open. Besides, we can see them coming from all directions."

"Do you have a rearview mirror in your sunglasses?" asked Marge, sounding grumpy.

"No, but my ears still work."

They'd picked a spot that backed up to an area of thick tropical plants and trees. Someone could ambush them from behind, but they'd make a racket crashing through the vegetation, and Delphine would be able to hear them from a mile away.

Marge looked behind their chairs. "I don't know…"

"Just enjoy this beautiful morning," said Delphine. "And keep your eyes peeled. They can see us, but that means we can maybe spot them too."

"Minka and Martin. What kind of name is Minka anyway?" asked Marge.

"I would imagine it's a Norwegian name," said Delphine, rolling her eyes.

"Minka and Martin. M and M. M&Ms. Now I'm hungry." Marge huffed and squirmed around in her chair some more.

Delphine yawned. "I really wish you had slept on the sofa bed last night. I pulled it out for you and everything."

"The sofa bed is uncomfortable," said Marge.

"How do you know? You've never slept on it!"

"If you think it's so great, you sleep on it."

Delphine scoffed. "It's my room."

"Okay," said Marge. "No need to get your swimsuit in a bind. The bed is plenty big for both of us, so maybe you need to lighten up a little."

"The bed is not big enough for both of us. You keep sleeping in the middle of it and stabbing me in the back with your bony knees," said Delphine.

Marge laughed. "You should be glad that's all I've been doing. I'm famous for being a nighttime cuddler."

"Lucky me," mumbled Delphine.

"Anyways, where's your boyfriend this morning?" asked Marge.

"He said he'll meet up with us at the club later this morning," said Delphine.

"Ha!" Marge pointed at her.

"What?"

Marge giggled. "You didn't deny he's your boyfriend!"

"I didn't? Well, I meant to." Delphine wondered why she'd forgotten to do that. Perhaps her memory was going.

She she was about two minutes from starting a fistfight with Marge, but it would have to wait. She spotted Brock Celery coming their way, carrying two tropical drinks.

"Babe!" said Brock, smiling at Marge. He put the drinks down on a nearby patio table, where the group had eaten breakfast earlier. He perused the plates and plucked a leftover piece of bacon from one. He popped it in his mouth and Delphine seethed. She'd been saving that piece of bacon.

"Oh, hi Brock," said Marge in a nonchalant tone.

Brock Celery dragged a chair from the table and placed it next to Marge. He brought the drinks over, handed one to Marge, and sat in the chair facing her.

"Babe, where were you last night?" Brock asked.

"Umm..." Marge shifted the icy glass from one hand to the other and back again.

Delphine couldn't wait to see what happened next.

"Well, no biggie," said Brock, and he slurped some of his icy, fruity drink, which presumably contained alcohol. It seemed a little too early in the morning even for day drinking, but it was a well-known fact movie stars could do whatever the heck they wanted.

"It's not?" asked Marge.

"Nah," said Brock. "It all turned out great. I wanted to thank you, actually!"

Marge put the drink down on the little table between her and Delphine. She was sporting an annoyed expression now, perhaps because it sounded like Brock hadn't missed her very much.

"You do?" Marge asked.

Brock slurped more tropical drink. "Uh-*huh*! Those ladies in room 202 turned out to be a whole lot of fun. In fact, I'm exhausted! I'm heading back to my room for a nap. Say, care to join me?" he leaned forward and started to reach for Marge's knee.

Marge slapped his hand away. "No, I do not want to 'nap' with you, Brock Celery. It just so happens I have a very nice boyfriend. So I think you should leave now."

"Oh yeah? If your boyfriend is so great, where is he?" Brock looked out at the bay and shaded his eyes with his hand for dramatic effect.

"He is right here," said Kenji from behind Brock's chair. "You heard her, she wants you to leave." He stood with his fists clenched at his sides.

Marge gasped. "Oh my!"

Even Delphine was impressed by the show of protectiveness.

Brock raised his hands, one holding his drink, the other giving Kenji an open palm, and stood up. "Okay, okay," he said. "Jeez. You don't have to be so uptight." He glared down at Marge, with a this-is-your-last-chance expression, but she turned away. "Your loss, babe. Anyway, I gotta go. I'm meeting up with the girls in 202 again later." He picked up the drink he'd brought for her and sauntered off.

"That was fun," said Delphine.

Kenji gave her a murderous glare. She smiled at him.

"Brock Celery is too big for his britches," said Marge.

"You're just jealous," said Delphine. "Until now, you thought he walked on water."

Marge tried to turn in her lounge chair to face Delphine but instead almost fell off it. "You are not helping right now."

Delphine formally decided her official capacity on the trip was to not help anyone. If her own life hadn't been dependent on the capture of the thieves, she'd seriously have considered walking away and leaving them to it.

Marge got up and sat next to Kenji on his chair. "Thank you for saving me, Kenji Bear," she said.

He hugged her back. "Anything for you, Super Babe."

Something caught Delphine's attention near the water. Minka and Martin stood out on the shore, talking with a few other people. It looked like they might be getting ready to start a paddleboarding lesson.

"I hate to break up this Hallmark moment, but we have company." Delphine casually tilted her head at the water.

"Oh," said Kenji when he caught sight of the Solbergs. "What are they doing here, I wonder."

"Oh, it's M&M," said Marge. "I thought they weren't staying in the bungalow."

"We're currently on the club's property, not the resort's. Maybe they have a membership." Delphine stood up and took off her glasses.

She looked at Kenji.

"Let's go," he said.

"You're just gonna leave me here?" barked Marge.

"Yes," said Delphine and Kenji. They set off at a slow walk and aimed for the group of people on the beach.

CHAPTER 35

Delphine and Kenji didn't make it within twenty yards of the paddleboard class before Minka and Martin Solberg spotted them and took off down the beach in the direction of the bungalows.

Delphine considered not pursuing them. They still had to contact Kenji if they wanted their money; why bother going after them now? But it had been instinct. A desire to get the situation handled sooner rather than later. And since Kenji didn't have the ransom money, surprise might work in their favor.

Kenji must've thought the same thing because he got the jump on her and ran off after the Norwegians at a healthy pace. She followed. Reluctantly.

Minka and Martin, being maybe thirty years younger, were faster than Kenji, but not by much; they were rather out of shape, thank goodness. Delphine brought up the back and couldn't help noticing Marge was not sitting under the palm trees where they'd left her. Great.

The siblings disappeared around a turn in the path, but she could still see Kenji. A few seconds later, someone yelled "Hi-*yah*!" from around the bend.

The someone sounded a lot like Marge. Delphine cursed under

her breath as she ran. When she rounded the corner, there stood Marge, bent over double and rubbing her knee.

"Managed to slow 'em down, but couldn't stop 'em," panted Marge.

"Good work," said Delphine, surprised she had an occasion on which to speak those words to Marge. "Now call Griffin as quick as you can and have her and Miko meet us at the beach in front of the bungalows." She resumed her slow run in pursuit of Kenji and the Norwegians.

"You got it, Big D!" yelled Marge.

Delphine passed one of the hotel pools. The chase had started to draw attention from some vacationers. Several people sitting in lounge chairs watched her pass and spoke to each other in low tones while pointing at her. She waved and continued on her way.

The path turned back toward the beach, and when she got closer to the bungalows, she caught sight of Minka and Martin paddling out into the bay in a two-person kayak. Kenji stood on the sand and watched them go.

"How did they get a kayak?" asked Delphine as she caught up to Kenji. She felt a little out of breath but not too bad, all things considered. At least she still had *some* aerobic capacity.

"The resort leaves paddleboards and little boats and stuff out during the day for guests to use." Kenji pointed to a paddleboard resting in the sand right in front of them.

"Oh," said Delphine, embarrassed she'd not noticed before.

"I need to go after them," said Kenji.

"I think so," said Delphine.

"To get them to give my laptop back."

"Right."

"And maybe I should apologize for killing their parents," said Kenji.

"We aren't necessarily responsible for the death of their parents."

"Okay, but we kind of are," said Kenji.

"We have no way of knowing for sure. It was complete chaos in that grocery store."

The Norwegians paddled farther out into the bay.

"You're wasting time." Delphine pointed to the paddleboard. "Didn't you take lessons?"

"I fell off it when we were still practicing on the sand," he said.

"Perfect." She pushed him toward the board.

"What?"

"You won't be using it on sand, you'll be on the water. It'll be fine." She picked up the oar and handed it to him. "Go."

Kenji dragged the board to the water, waded in, and climbed on. He paddled a few times and slapped the water with his oar. "I don't have a life vest," he shouted.

"Oh for crying out loud," she shouted back.

A little farther down the shore sat a one-person kayak. She should've made Kenji use it, but too late now. She ran to it, pushed it into the water, hopped in, and took off. Within minutes she'd passed Kenji and was gaining on the two-person kayak, which was still gliding out into the bay. Where the siblings intended to go, Delphine had no idea. It seemed ridiculous to flee a Hawaiian island by way of a kayak.

"I'm coming!" yelled Kenji from somewhere behind her.

Try as she might, the distance between her kayak and the Solbergs' began to grow. Things were not heading in the right direction. She needed to catch up with them and have a little chat to persuade them to return the laptop. Neither she nor Kenji could afford to let that computer get into the wrong hands, if it wasn't already too late.

"We're coming too!" shouted another voice behind her. The shout was accompanied by a faint whining sound.

Delphine didn't want to spare a single second from paddling to turn to see what might be happening behind her, but she couldn't resist. A small dinghy with the tiniest outboard motor imaginable had passed Kenji and was gaining on her. Marge sat in the helm and Griffin sat in the stern, in charge of steering the boat.

"We got this!" said Marge as their vessel got closer.

But Delphine wasn't so sure. Both Norwegians still paddled at a furious pace, hardly creating a splash as they cut through the water. They didn't seem to be tiring, even though she'd taken them to be terribly out of shape. They simply had more energy—just another perk of being so much younger.

Before she knew it, Griffin and Marge had passed her by and were putt-putting their way across the bay. Even so, their target pulled farther away. How could that be!

"We're going to lose them!" she shouted into the offshore breeze.

"No we won't!" yelled yet another voice, this one behind her. It was accompanied by a throaty growl.

Again Delphine turned and this time discovered Kapuni Jones's *Fancy Feast* had joined the chase.

"What on earth!" yelled Delphine.

Kapuni and Miko waved from the bow and Kenji waved from the side of the boat; he must've gotten picked up. Delphine spotted Momi high in the bridge wearing a maniacally gleeful grin.

The yacht slowed down and Kenji disappeared to the back of the boat.

She was the next target.

The yacht pulled up beside her and Delphine paddled for the stern, where Kenji waited for her. He caught the front of the kayak and she climbed onto the boat's diving platform, where she was greeted by Kapuni. He and Kenji pulled the kayak aboard the yacht. Kapuni let out a wolf whistle after which Momi shot off after Griffin and Marge.

"How did you get here so fast?" Delphine asked Kapuni. There was no way he could have made it from the marina to this part of the bay, just in the time since she'd told Marge to call Griffin and Miko.

"I was on my way to the resort," said Kapuni over the rumble of the engine, which Momi had started to push harder. "I was gonna go fishing and thought maybe I could see you out on the beach." He grinned at her. "I want to catch you in your bikini."

And she'd sort of been watching for his boat all morning. "I don't own a bikini," she said, trying to sound affronted.

Momi caught up with Marge and Griffin and repeated the pick-up process. Kenji tied the dinghy to the back of the yacht as the two women came on board. Kapuni let out another piercing whistle and again Momi gunned the engine.

The Solbergs' little kayak would be easy prey now. It had almost reached a sandbar, halfway out into the bay.

"We got 'em," now, said Kapuni, rubbing his hands together in anticipation.

"What are we going to do when we get 'em?" asked Marge.

Kapuni looked at Delphine with excitement. "Do we get to do some strong-arming?"

"No," said Kenji in a calm voice. "I will take care of this."

The kayak arrived at the sandbar and Minka and Martin stopped paddling. They got out of the little vessel and stood knee-deep in the water.

"It's like they're waiting for us," said Griffin.

Delphine scanned the bay. "They're waiting, but not for us." She pointed to their left, where a small, sleek speedboat skimmed the turquoise water on a direct course for the sandbar.

"Momi!" Kapuni yelled.

The yacht's engines roared louder ,and the boat surged under their feet.

But the speedboat was faster. It slowed down as it neared the sandbar, long enough for Minka and Martin Solberg to jump in, head-first. In seconds, they were gone.

The yacht slowed down and Momi made a wide arc to head back to the resort.

"That was a real letdown," said Marge.

"Agreed," said Kapuni.

"It was kind of fun though," said Griffin.

Marge giggled. "I'll say!"

"Did you recognize the speedboat?" Delphine asked Kapuni.

"Nope," he said.

She squinted at him, giving him her best skeptical look.

He threw up his hands. "What! I don't know every single boat on the whole stupid island!"

Kenji had been checking his phone but now his eyes swung to Delphine's. "I got a text."

She held out her hand and he gave her his phone. She read the message out loud. "That was an insufferably stupid move. Our demand has risen to $3,000,000. 4:00 p.m., alley behind Kaimoa Bay SuperTarget."

Everyone stood there thinking about the text. Delphine gave Kenji his phone back.

"That's dumb," said Marge.

"I can't get the money," said Kenji. His voice sounded thin and helpless. "

"That's why it's dumb," said Marge. "Give me your phone."

"I would advise against it," Delphine told Kenji.

He stared at Delphine as he dropped the phone into Marge's outstretched palm. Delphine rolled her eyes.

"We have done it our way for years," he said.

"Yes, and it's worked for years," she said.

Kenji took a deep breath. "Well now it is time to try new things, isn't it."

As they argued, Marge tapped out a message on Kenji's phone.

"Maybe you can call Frances again," said Delphine. "Or request an extension."

"This is not the IRS we're talking about," said Kenji. He huffed.

Kapuni turned to Griffin. "I can't wait to see where this goes."

"It's better than the movies," agreed Griffin.

Delphine peered over Marge's shoulder. "Let me read what you've written."

"No," said Marge, moving away from her.

The phone dinged, and Marge scanned the message and laughed. "Okay, now you can read it."

They crowded around the screen.

Kenji: That's nutso, u idiots. It will take me 2 more days to get that kind of cheddar. And r u sure u want to give me 2 more days to cratch your stupid butts? U can have your 2mil today at 4—that works better 4 me.

555-555-5555: Fine. But you had better be careful and don't do anything to make us angrier.

"Is cratching your butt like a combo of scratching and catching?" asked Kapuni. "I like it."

CHAPTER 36

Momi maneuvered Kapuni's yacht as close to the shore as she could, and Miko drove everyone the rest of the way to the beach in the tiny dinghy Griffin had appropriated from the resort. An hour later, Kenji sat slumped in a chair under a shade umbrella by the club's salt-water pool. He'd probably never see his laptop again, and that now looked like a best-case scenario. He was supposed to meet with Minka and Martin Solberg that afternoon to hand over two million dollars he didn't have, after telling them in a text that he did have it. Or at least Marge had told them.

He'd called Frances again, but she couldn't do much. She told him she could maybe get a little money wired to the local bank, but not nearly enough to placate angry laptop thieves with a craving for vengeance.

Maybe he should try to explain everything to the Solbergs. It wasn't like he could pull millions of dollars out of his—well, he couldn't come up with that kind of money out of thin air.

But the icing on the whole crap cake, assuming he'd get out of the afternoon's meeting alive, would be getting fired. He had enjoyed still having access to the Falls. Helping out from time to time made him feel vital and needed. And the older he got, the less often he felt vital and needed. Maybe that was why he loved

Marge; it was nice to have someone who counted on you. And extra nice to have someone to count on.

He watched Marge and Delphine swim in the pool. His two best friends were willing to do almost anything to help him out. How had he gotten so lucky? He pretended he had dust in his eye and wiped away a tear.

It was 11:00 a.m. They still had a few hours until he had to meet the Norwegians. When his friends got out of the pool they'd have some lunch, then he'd mentally prepare himself to head to the designated location. Marge and Delphine had said they wanted to go along, but he wasn't convinced taking them for backup would be a good idea. Maybe he should leave early. He could keep them out of it if he snuck away now; they'd done enough already. But it wouldn't work. They knew the time and place of the transaction and would show up anyway.

His phone pinged with a text. It was the real estate agent Kapuni Jones had referred him to. Kenji had big plans—what better way to show Marge he cared than to buy a condo on the island so they could visit anytime they wanted? Of course it would be a two-bedroom place. That way she could have her own room until she felt comfortable enough to share one with him. And once she was, they'd have a guest room so they could invite visitors. Like Delphine.

He read the text. The agent had forwarded several listings for him to consider. He'd get to them later this afternoon, provided everything went okay with the laptop exchange. Maybe he could have Delphine keep Marge occupied so he could go look at the most promising units. Or maybe he'd buy one anyway, sight unseen, and surprise Marge with the news once they were back in Los Angeles. He vowed to sell all his crypto when the market recovered and invest more in real estate instead.

Griffin walked up to the table and pointed to the chair next to him. "May I?"

He gave her a weak smile. "Of course. You never need to ask."

"I'm sorry it didn't work out going after those guys," she said as she sat down.

"It was a dumb idea," said Kenji. "But well intended."

"What's their deal?" asked Griffin. "What's the point of this whole thing?"

"Your grandmother and I were at least partially responsible for the death of their parents during one of our missions."

Griffin sighed. "No one likes it when a job goes sideways. We're all trained to avoid it, but sometimes it just happens. But I don't have to tell you."

"Definitely not," said Kenji. "It sounds like you saw some action."

"Not really. You don't get out much when you're in the forensic accounting department. But I watch a lot of TV," said Griffin. "What kind of mission was it, where their parents got killed?"

"There was an unscrupulous group of fish traders based out of Norway, who price-gouged the international herring market for decades. We thought we had a good handle on taking them out, but the last operation went so badly, our agency shut us down and sent us home."

Griffin shook her head. "There are so many ways human beings are lousy to each other. You would think we could all agree on something as harmless as fish."

"As long as there are opportunities to take advantage of someone, there will always be herring mafias," said Kenji, feeling very wise.

"Are they still in operation?" asked Griffin.

"I have no idea. And I don't have my laptop so I can't check."

"Why did they take your laptop anyway? Why not just kill you, for revenge?"

Kenji frowned. "That is a good question. Maybe I will ask them this afternoon."

Delphine got out of the pool and headed their way. He'd

always marveled at how poised she was. She'd always be his best friend.

"Your grandmother has done so much good in this world over her lifetime," Kenji said to Griffin. "I am sorry I have dragged her back into a world where people do bad and stupid things. She deserves better."

"Well now I'm depressed," said Griffin.

Kenji was too. "Sorry."

Griffin said, "I came over to let you know Minka and Martin have checked out of the resort."

"They have?" Delphine appeared at the table, wrapped in a giant beach towel.

"Yup," said Griffin.

Delphine retrieved her tote bag from the back of a chair and pulled out the calling card with the line drawing of a fishing boat. She sat down at the table and looked at the phone number.

"That reminds me," said Griffin, pointing to the card. "Miko traced that number. It's a burner, as expected."

Delphine nodded. "I figured. But it was nice of him to check. Miko's a fine young man."

"I guess," said Griffin.

She and Delphine burst out laughing.

"What is so funny?" asked Kenji.

"It's just… I mean… Grandma?" Griffin said.

"She was being sarcastic," said Delphine. "Miko is very nice, and a very good-looking man."

"Oh." Kenji didn't have much bandwidth for girl-talk about guys, even on his good days.

They fell quiet. Delphine turned the calling card over. She studied the drawing of the fishing boat, and Kenji studied her. He recognized the expression on her face and felt a sudden glimmer of hope. "You have a plan, don't you."

Delphine smiled.

CHAPTER 37

Delphine checked her hair one last time in the bathroom mirror. As expected, Marge had managed to eventually create utter chaos in her Zen-like bathroom suite. Jumpsuits and bras hung everywhere, along with towels, swimsuits, and for some reason, a pair of blue-striped tube socks. No one she knew, including Kenji, wore tube socks, so who they belonged to was anyone's guess.

She took a deep breath as she looked at her reflection. Was she too old to be chasing bad guys around? Was there a definitive answer to that question? What would she rather be doing?

In any case, she didn't have much of a say in the matter. Something always came up that was so dire, the only choice was to act.

She fixed her hair again and thought of Kapuni's dimples and twinkling eyes. She couldn't help it.

Her phone buzzed with a text message. Kapuni was waiting for her in front of the resort. She texted back, saying she was on her way.

As she walked through the grounds to the lobby, she wondered one more time whether it had been a bad idea to involve Kapuni in her plan. The facts suggested a 50-50 chance he was not someone they would want help from. But her gut told her otherwise. The blending of logic and instinct led her to seek his help. Whatever happened next was all just part of the game.

Five minutes later, the two of them sat in the back seat of his Mercedes as Momi raced along the streets. Delphine gripped the door handle and held on for dear life. Kapuni seemed perfectly at ease, and bounced around on the seat as his driver took the turns.

"Does she have many speeding tickets?" asked Delphine in a low voice.

Kapuni shook his head. "She has a preternatural sense for speed traps."

Delphine pointed to the backpack on the floor between them. "I'm guessing you have everything we need in there?"

"That is a very existential question," he said. "But I brought Lucinda, if that's what you mean."

She looked pointedly at his bare feet. "We might need to do some running."

"Have you ever tried barefoot running? It's invigorating!" He peered down at her shoes—a pair of sensible espadrilles. "You should wear shoes less often. Much better for your feet."

"If we make it through all this, and I actually get a day or two of something resembling a vacation, I'll give it a try."

Kapuni pointed his index finger at her. "I'm going to hold you to it." He squinted one eye and adjusted the other fingers on his hand until he was pointing a literal hand gun at her. "Peew-peew."

Delphine let out an exhale she didn't know she'd been holding. Maybe this man's weirdness was exactly what she needed in her life. Provided he wasn't contributing to her untimely demise.

Momi pulled into a parking spot at the Kaimoa Bay Marina with the precision of a pilot landing a 777. Delphine wondered if Momi also flew planes.

The car faced the entrance to the docks and had a clear path to the exit.

"Thank you my dear," Kapuni said to Momi. "As always, I'm

sorry it's over." He took his pistol and a piece of paper out of the backpack. He handed the gun to Delphine. "Be nice to Lucinda."

Delphine stretched her neck after their sudden stop and put the pistol in her purse.

All three of them got out of the car. Momi gave them a silent salute and leaned against the hood to wait. Delphine and Kapuni made their way to the marina entrance.

Delphine slung her purse across her torso to wear as a crossbody bag, in case they had to get someplace fast. In fact, she was counting on having to get somewhere fast. Kapuni handed her the piece of paper he'd taken from his backpack. On it he'd written a slip number: B217.

"Do you know where this is?" she asked him.

"I know the general direction," he said, and pointed to the wooden dock leading to the right.

"Thank you for following up on my hunch and getting this information for us," she said.

"Of course. The guy who owns the marina is a friend of mine."

"Friend or business associate?" asked Delphine.

"Sure," said Kapuni.

As they went, Kapuni checked all the signs to make sure they were still heading for slip B217. Delphine scanned all the boats they passed, keeping an eye out for anything that didn't look—or feel—quite right.

"It's right up there." Kapuni pointed to a narrower dock leading farther out into the marina.

Delphine stopped walking to gather herself together. "Okay, just like we discussed. Ready?"

Before she knew what was happening, Kapuni took her by the shoulders, brought her close, and gave her a kiss on the cheek. She didn't pull away.

"For luck," he said. "All on the up-and-up." He let go of her and raised his hands in innocence.

A million things went through her mind all at once. Surprise at Kapuni's forwardness. Guilt at not having stopped it immediately.

Flattered by the attention. Then guilt again. She thought of Charles.

"Normally if someone did that to me, I'd let them have it in the family jewels," said Delphine, still trying to overcome her shock.

He grinned his shark grin. "But you like me."

She laughed. "I guess I do. But liking you is different from trusting you. Now let's go."

"If you didn't trust me, it would be really stupid to be here with me right now. Just saying."

"I…"

"You trust me, you trust me!" Kapuni said in a sing-song voice.

"You can shut up now," said Delphine.

"I love it when you're bossy."

They went down another wooden walkway and stopped when they got to slip 217. A beat-up old fishing boat had been backed into the spot. Paint peeled off the wooden railings and as the vessel bobbed in the small waves, something in the hull squeaked, creating a pathetic, forlorn sound. The boat appeared abandoned. But that didn't mean it was.

"I expected to see the speedboat," said Kapuni, genuinely surprised.

"The speedboat belongs to someone else," she explained. "Someone they could call in a pinch. Maybe the nice gentlemen in the bungalow own it."

Kapuni didn't say anything for a few seconds. "Well, what a hunk of junk."

"A shit bucket, perhaps?" she asked.

Again he didn't say anything right away. "Ohhhhh, I get it now."

"Anyway," said Delphine, "I have a feeling that eyesore right there is Minka and Martin's primary residence."

"I don't know…" Kapuni sounded unconvinced. Delphine

didn't blame him, it was all just a theory until she had a little more to work with. Which she would hopefully have soon.

"Are you sure we shouldn't be wearing bulletproof vests?" whispered Kapuni.

"Too late now."

"Ha ha! Too late! You are so funny."

"Stop distracting me," said Delphine.

"Sorry."

Delphine moved slowly over to the gangplank leading onto the old boat. "Hello on board!" she said in a loud voice. "My, this place is a dump."

Martin's head popped out from the cabin door. His mouth hung open in shock, making his round head look like a surprised-face emoji. Minka's head appeared next to his—a second, more surprised emoji.

"We want the laptop now," said Delphine.

The siblings whispered to each other, but Delphine couldn't catch any of their conversation.

"We thought we'd save you a trip to SuperTarget," she added.

"Where is Kenji?" asked Martin in his tidy Northern-European English.

Delphine held up her hands. "We're just the money people. Do you want it or not?"

Martin looked from her to Kapuni, who had left his backpack in the car. Neither of them carried anything capable of holding a substantial amount of cash.

"Where is it?" asked Minka.

"We left it in the car," said Delphine. "We weren't sure you'd be in. But since you are..."

Minka and Martin conferred again.

"We would prefer to wait for our arranged meeting time," said Martin.

Delphine smiled. "Perhaps I didn't make myself as clear as I should have. You don't have another option. If you want your money, you'll come with us to the parking lot. And don't forget to bring the laptop." She turned on her heel and she and Kapuni walked back down the dock the way they'd come.

"Do you think it'll work?" Kapuni whispered.

Delphine tried to sound braver than she felt. "I think we'll be fine."

Kapuni interlaced his arm with hers and they strolled along the dock. "This would be nice if I weren't so concerned about getting shot in the back," he said.

CHAPTER 38

Delphine was pretty sure Minka and Martin had left their junky boat and were a few minutes behind them on the walkway. But she couldn't be positive without turning back, and she didn't want to do give them the satisfaction if they were watching her. She'd thought about installing Griffin or Miko as a lookout somewhere along their walk, but it hadn't been feasible.

"What makes you so sure they're desperate for cash?" asked Kapuni.

"If they weren't," said Delphine, "I imagine Kenji and I would be dead by now. They want revenge for their parents' deaths, but they want money more. What they need it for, I have no idea. My theory might be a bit of a gamble, but so far it's working."

"Everything's a gamble in the end," said Kapuni.

Delphine shuddered at the astuteness of his words.

They made it to the Mercedes. Momi had gotten back in behind the wheel and sat watching them approach with an inscrutable gaze. Delphine and Kapuni stood in front of the car and waited for their quarry. A moment later, the Solberg siblings huffed and puffed their way into the parking lot.

"What if they don't have their car keys with them?" asked Kapuni.

Delphine laughed. "Then I guess we are screwed, as Kenji likes to say. I appreciate you considering this from all angles but trust me on this one."

"If you say so…" He didn't sound very sure, but Delphine didn't mind.

Minka and Martin stopped about ten yards in front of the Mercedes. Kapuni walked to the back passenger door and Delphine moved to the front passenger door.

"Do you have the laptop?" Delphine called out.

Minka pointed to the messenger bag hanging from her shoulder.

Delphine shook her head. "I want to see it."

Minka rolled her eyes but lifted the flap on the bag and removed the laptop. Delphine spotted the CougarWear sticker on the front. Definitely Kenji's.

"Now the money," said Minka.

"I was mistaken," said Delphine as she opened car door. "We forgot the money, sorry!"

Martin pulled a revolver from the waistband of his pants. Delphine had hoped firearms wouldn't be necessary, but one always had to be prepared. "Are you ready, Momi?" she said quietly.

Momi started the Mercedes. Kapuni got in the back seat.

"Hand it over," said Martin.

"I told you, we don't have it," said Delphine.

Minka drew a gun from her bag and pointed it at the car. "Then you will pay. Martin, I told you this was a bad idea. We should have killed her and the Yamamoto man when we had the chance."

"Føttene dine lukter råtten sild!" yelled Delphine. She got into the car and rolled down the window. Momi put the Mercedes into drive, and they rolled slowly toward the parking lot exit.

"Ok det gjør det!" Minka said to Martin. She held up what looked like a ring of keys, and the siblings ran for a nearby car.

Delphine and Kapuni watched out the back window as Minka got behind the wheel of a shiny blue Honda Civic.

Momi also had her eye the Norwegians in her rearview mirror.

"Can you handle them?" Delphine asked.

Momi's face flashed a lopsided devilish grin, and she pulled out into traffic.

"What did you say to them?" Kapuni asked Delphine as they raced down the street.

"Something you don't want to say to someone in the Herring Mafia," she told him.

CHAPTER 39

The Honda Civic turned out to be faster than anyone in Kapuni's Mercedes had anticipated, and Delphine began to worry. Minka wasn't a half-bad driver either. The speed and route of the car chase was hampered by traffic, but surprisingly, not many stoplights, and the ones they did encounter stayed green. The Civic remained on their tail.

"Momi, that Norwegian is competition for you," Kapuni said from the back seat, laughing. Momi ignored him and swerved at the last possible second into a lane leading onto a highway.

Delphine checked the map app on her phone and oriented herself. Their route would take them around the southern tip of the island, known for a stretch of sheer cliffs and high winds. And a very twisty road. She took hold of the suicide handle above the car door.

A check of the side mirror indicated the Norwegians were still riding their bumper. They were so close, Delphine could see Minka's angry scowl behind the Civic's windshield. Momi gripped the leather steering wheel tighter, adjusted her neck and shoulders, and pressed harder on the gas pedal. The Mercedes lurched ahead, like a big, excited dog let off his leash. Delphine put her phone in her lap so she could grip the side of her seat as well as the suicide handle.

"Woohoo!" said Kapuni from the back. "We need to do this more often!"

"Do you mean high-speed chases in general, or trying to escape from angry kidnappers specifically?" Delphine asked.

"Yes!" said Kapuni.

Delphine had to admit she agreed. The adrenaline rush was addictive—it always had been. She felt young again, although also grateful that Momi was behind the wheel instead of herself.

The road got more twisty, and Momi had to let off the gas occasionally in order to make the turns. In a few places she took even more liberties with their lives and passed slower cars by darting into the lane of oncoming traffic. The Civic was still right behind them.

"That car must be modified," said Delphine. "Are you sure you can do this, Momi?"

Momi smirked and kept driving.

The highway took them higher into the mountains. If the scenery hadn't been a blur, Delphine reckoned she'd be able to see the resort, way down below, in the center of the U-shaped bay. Somewhere down there was a lone lounge chair under a palm tree, waiting for her.

Oh well.

A sharp *pop!* pierced the air and Delphine was no longer able to check the side mirror—it had been shot off. Momi growled and drove faster.

Delphine tried to lean around her seat to peer out the back window, but they took the turns so fast now she couldn't keep her head steady. She gave up and faced the front.

They passed a sign for an upcoming exit; in a half mile they'd get to a scenic overlook of the bay. They were almost to the highest point on the highway.

The Norwegians fired at the car again and the bullet hit the back window. With great effort Delphine kept low and managed to peer around the seat. Kapuni lay sideways on the back seat and his head was close to hers.

"Bulletproof glass," he said. "A good investment for my—" he cut himself off.

"You were going to say, in your line of work, weren't you," said Delphine.

He nodded.

An image flashed in her head of the Mercedes exiting at the overlook, and the two cars coming to a stop with everyone, including Momi and Kapuni, getting out and pointing guns at her. She knew her plan had left a lot of leeway for things to go wrong, for betrayal and backstabbing even. The tables could've been turned on her at any point so far though, and they hadn't, so that gave her some comfort. But the game wasn't over yet. With every curve in the road, she was putting her trust in Kapuni Jones. He was a mystery that needed to be solved, only maybe not while they were being shot at. But soon.

Momi took the exit for the overlook at least fifty miles over the recommended speed posted on the yellow caution sign.

"They're still behind us," Kapuni informed them.

The offramp let out into a big parking lot. A huge white touring bus sat at the far end. The words *FALL-AWAY TOURS* in big red letters took up the length of the coach. An ironic name, considering they were parked at the top of a very high, and very sheer, cliff.

A few other cars dotted the lot, maybe ten at most, plus one van. A group of tourists all wearing white baseball caps were walking down the path leading to the overlook. But most of the lot was empty and Momi took advantage of the space.

The Mercedes sped up and Delphine grabbed for both the door handle and suicide handle. Momi slammed on the brakes and the car began to drift. It turned 180 degrees and came to a screeching stop facing the way they'd come in. The Civic had to slow so fast it first banked sideways, then came to rest thirty feet in front of them with the grille facing the Mercedes.

Martin jumped out of the car with his gun pointed at them. "Ute!" he screamed.

"I think I understood that one," said Kapuni.

He, Delphine, and Momi slowly climbed out of the car and raised their arms in the air.

Delphine clenched her jaw, and her eyes darted around the lot as she tried to assess their situation. They weren't in the best position to bargain. Heat built up under her blazer and she flexed her hands to relieve the tension. She guessed she had a few more seconds to come up with something.

And a few seconds later, another car tore into the lot—a white Toyota SUV. It stopped behind the Civic with more screeching tires, and blocked everyone in. Delphine took the opportunity to pull Kapuni's gun from her pocket and point it at Martin.

Now a third car, a silver Chevy sedan, entered the lot at a much slower pace and came to a tidy halt on Delphine's right, halfway between the Mercedes and the Civic, nose pointed inward at the action to create a triangle of front ends. The left side between the Mercedes and the Civic was open, but that part of the lot backed up to a dense area of trees and bushes followed a few feet back by a sheer mountainside, going up and up and disappearing into a bank of misty clouds.

Kenji emerged from the passenger side of the Chevy. He'd stuffed a gun into the waistband of his shorts, but didn't draw it. Marge waved at Delphine from behind the steering wheel and stayed in the car.

Wind howled around them, and Delphine's short hair stood up straight.

By this time, Minka had gotten out of the Honda with her messenger bag across her chest. Delphine and Martin stood with guns pointing at each other.

"Time to hand over my laptop," said Kenji.

"Time for you to hand over the money," said Martin.

Kenji walked forward a few steps, trying to keep his hair, which he'd been letting grow longer, from whipping around his face and eyes. He opened his mouth to say something but a lock of hair just long enough to cause trouble across his eyes and he pawed at his face to remove it.

The Solberg siblings took advantage of the distraction and made a break for it. They shot past the Chevy. Delphine tracked them with her pistol, but didn't shoot. There weren't many places Martin and Minka could go—they certainly weren't leaving the area on foot.

The two headed straight for the path to the scenic overhang.

"Let's go!" said Kenji, and he took off after them. Miko and Griffin, who had come around the Civic and saw what was happening, ran after Kenji. Delphine and Kapuni followed. Momi had been instructed to stay with the Mercedes and like the good driver she was, complied and got back into the car. Delphine hoped Marge would stay in the Chevy as she'd been instructed but doubted it would happen.

The Solberg siblings had a decent lead on their pursuers. But where would they go? They were literally headed for the edge of a cliff.

When Delphine and Kapuni caught up to the action, Minka and Martin had made it to the edge of the overhang. A four-foot-high cement wall had been constructed along the length of the overlook to prevent anyone from falling, and the siblings stood with their backs to the bay, watching everyone catch up and surround them. The wind came from the direction of the water and blew Minka's shoulder-length brown hair into her face. She kept trying to tuck the wild strands behind her ears, but it was probably a hopeless battle. Delphine leaned forward and the breeze was so strong, it kept her standing upright.

Minka reached into her bag and pulled out Kenji's laptop.

"Stay back everyone!" said Kenji, holding his arms out to keep them all behind him.

The group of tourists, had been wandering around the open space, taking pictures of the bay and selfies of themselves along the stone wall. They took off their white caps to let their hair fly everywhere, and snapped photos, laughing at the results. But once Kenji shouted his warning, they finally realized they might be in danger. One of them, presumably the tour leader, spoke in hushed and hurried Japanese to his wards. They all put their hats back on and hurried to leave the outlook. As they passed her, Delphine caught a glimpse of the writing on their caps: *HAPPY KITTY TOURS AND BOBA CAFÉ*. She turned around in time to see a few of the stragglers stopped to take pictures of the unfolding drama.

Martin pointed his weapon at Kenji, and Minka held the laptop out over the cement wall. The wind kept catching the thin, flat device, and it flapped around wildly in the air as Minka tried to hang onto it. Everyone gasped as she almost lost her grip.

"What did I miss?" yelled Marge, coming to a stop next to Delphine.

Martin and Minka craned to see around Kenji, and everyone else turned their way too. Marge waved and smiled as she tried to catch her breath.

"You just couldn't do as we asked, could you," whispered Delphine.

"I figured you might need the extra muscle, in case things got ugly," Marge whispered back.

Everyone refocused on Minka and Martin.

"Sorry about that," said Kenji. "Now, where were we?"

"If you want your computer back, you will hand over the money and give us safe passage from this scenic overlook," said Martin. He had to yell over the howl of the wind.

"First I would like to say that Delphine and I are sorry for the loss of your parents," said Kenji.

Martin held the gun with both hands now, the barrel pointed at Kenji's chest. "We don't believe you. It is all your fault we had to go live with our Uncle Frode. He was a real jerk, you know."

"I am sorry about that too," said Kenji, raising his hands. His gun stayed tucked into his waistband. "I hate to tell you this, but some of your own people might have taken out your parents. The type of weapon they were shot with was never discovered. I believe there may have been a cover-up in your Herring Mafia."

Martin and Minka spoke to each other in hushed Norwegian.

"No!" shouted Minka. "We do not believe you; you're trying to confuse us. It's your fault!"

"If you don't believe me, I suppose you could kill me to get your revenge. But you know, revenge is never a good idea. Action taken from a place of anger is not right action."

More whispering in Norwegian. Delphine couldn't make any of it out.

"Now you are talking nonsense," yelled Martin.

Kenji shrugged.

"Give us the money!" screamed Minka, sounding desperate now.

Martin lunged forward a step, and Kapuni and Miko came up from behind Kenji to stand next to him. Each of them held pistols aimed at Minka and Martin.

"Why do you need it so badly?" asked Kenji.

Martin rolled his eyes, like Kenji was a little slow. But he answered the question, to Kenji's surprise. "My sister and I are planning to take over the Herring Mafia. Only we're tired of the weather in Norway. We want to expand into warmer places and need seed money."

"How did you recognize us in the first place?" asked Kenji.

"You and your girlfriend—"

"Now when you say girlfriend, to you mean me or her?" Marge yelled over the wind. She pointed first to herself, then to Delphine.

"You don't have to answer that," Delphine yelled at Martin.

"Oh gosh, thank you, you old bat," said Minka with a sneer.

"I want to know how you recognized us," said Kenji, trying to keep his cool.

"No more questions!" screamed Martin. "But if you must know, you people—all three of you—are not very subtle. We heard you at the pool. It was easy to put your names in context with a *special laptop.*" He made a jeering face and shifted his weight side to side, mocking Kenji.

"He's very wordy for someone who didn't want to answer any more questions," Kapuni said to Kenji.

"Quiet!" said Minka and flapped the laptop around in the air a few more times. "Money!"

Martin kept his gun pointed at Kenji's chest and held out his other hand, palm-up.

"Explain to me how this is going work," yelled Kenji.

"Well," said Martin, trying to think it through. "You will hand me two million dollars, and I will hand you your laptop. You and your friends will move over to the cliff wall over there and wait until my sister and I have safely left the parking lot." He pointed the gun to a sheer wall of rock to Delphine's left, then back at Kenji.

"it's kind of windy out here," said Kenji. "I can't just hand you a bunch of money. What should I put it in?"

"You give it to us in whatever bag you brought it in," said Minka in a voice implying Kenji was a little dim.

Kenji sighed. "I don't know, it sounds complicated."

"Then I will—plech!" Minka stopped talking to pull some hair out of her mouth. "Then I will drop this!" she shouted as she waved the laptop again.

Kenji crossed his arms. "Okay, go ahead."

The siblings appeared dumbfounded. Kenji took a few steps in their direction.

"I mean it!" Minka held the computer farther out over the expanse of nothingness behind the wall.

"Did you download what was on it?" Kenji asked, taking another step forward.

Martin looked embarrassed. "We tried to guess your password but got locked out."

"I see," said Kenji. "So you don't have the data stored anywhere. But it doesn't matter, since it was only a bargaining tool to get money."

"Well … yes," said Martin.

Neither Kenji nor Martin had to shout anymore, they stood so close. Martin still had his gun aimed at Kenji's chest, but doubt and fear had begun to make his hand shake.

Kenji shrugged. "I don't feel like paying you. So go ahead and let it drop."

"What?" said Martin, sounding bewildered by Kenji's response.

"Well, it doesn't really matter to me. If you drop it, you lose all the information. And I just have to get a new laptop. Not much of a problem from my point of view."

The Norwegians stood there, not able to decide what to do next.

"Go on," said Kenji.

CHAPTER 40

Kenji should have been happy and relieved that instead of letting his laptop fly off the side of a cliff, Minka Solberg stepped away from the wall and gingerly placed it in his hands. Well, Kenji was happy and relieved, but also kind of sad, now it was all over. He probably didn't have very many more adventures to enjoy in whatever time he had left. And he knew he would need to resign from consulting for the Falls.

Much to his surprise, a group of five men dressed in black and wearing Kevlar vests swarmed onto the scene. They disarmed Martin, who didn't seem to put up a fight of any kind, and handcuffed the siblings. Martin and Minka were led away before Kenji could say *last hurrah*.

Kenji whirled around to ask Delphine who had called the Falls, and ran right into his boss, Irene Roquefort, the new manager of the Southern California branch office. Agent Roquefort was a rather stocky woman and Kenji bounced off her Kevlar vest, which covered the torso of a dark-blue blazer. She wore her black hair pulled back in a severe bun, but she had a kind face, and it softened her appearance. A little bit.

"Nice work, Yamamoto," said Roquefort, and Kenji couldn't tell if she'd meant it sarcastically or not. She looked around the group—Delphine, Griffin, Miko, Kapuni, and Marge. "Quite a team you have here."

Now Kenji knew for sure she was being sarcastic. None of his friends were supposed to know about his work laptop, yet here they all were. He wanted to defend himself—*her boss* was the one who had insisted he take care of some work on his vacation; Bing had been the one to request Kenji research some old status reports from the '90s. But anything Kenji said now would only sound like an excuse. He hung his head and handed his computer over to his boss.

Roquefort tucked the laptop under one arm walked up to Delphine. "Hello Delphine, it's nice to finally meet you, I've heard very good things."

Delphine stayed as cool as ever. "Thanks for the offer, but no."

Roquefort laughed and tried to push her hair behind her ears as the wind tore at her tidy hairdo. "I had to try. We could use your expertise." Her eyes swung to the path leading to the parking lot. Director Bing and a black-clad agent walked their way.

"Hughes, please take those four back to the bus and debrief them," said Bing as he came to a stop in front of Kenji. Director Bing was a tall, balding man of about sixty, who, lucky for him, still looked good in a dark suit.

"Come with me please," the woman in black said, waving for Miko, Griffin, Kapuni, and Marge to follow her.

Bing smiled as Kapuni passed him by. "Jones. Howzit?"

Kapuni grinned his white-toothed smile and said, "Aloha, Bing. All good."

Kenji's jaw dropped and he heard Delphine gasp. Well, at least he hadn't been the only one shocked at the reveal.

"Wait, what?" asked Griffin. Even Miko appeared confused.

"Ma'am, this way," the black-clad agent said, with more force this time.

Griffin kept quiet and joined the agent, along with Marge and Miko.

Kapuni had been the one to bring in the agents and Kenji's manager. And the director of the Western States Division.

"Um," said Kenji. He looked at Kapuni who had a sheepish expression on his face.

Delphine remained speechless and the two friends shared a what-the-heck-is-happening moment while Kapuni Jones made small talk with Roquefort and Bing. Kenji sidled over to Delphine, and they stood watching the socializing spectacle together.

"I guess I better go check on my nephew and the others," said Kapuni, wrapping up his chat. "Good to see you both. Irene, tell your husband I said the Dodgers rule." The three of them shook hands. Kapuni Jones smiled at Delphine and disappeared down the path after the others.

"Now, you two," said Director Bing as he turned to Kenji and Delphine. The breeze hit him sideways, and the strands of his combover flew in the wrong direction. "You will be receiving special commendations for apprehending two members of the Herring Mafia, Minka and Martin Solberg."

"Oh, that is nice, thank you," said Kenji, surprised.

"And of course Kenji, you're fired," added Bing.

Kenji nodded. "That part is not nice, but fair."

"Is the Herring Mafia still active?" Delphine asked.

"Yes, I'm afraid so. But their power has weakened, and competition from other parts of the world has loosened the organization's grasp on the supply chain. We think the Solbergs have been trying to expand into other markets."

"You've been watching them," said Delphine.

"They've been on our radar, but we didn't know they were here until Jones told us," said Roquefort. "And he says you're the one who put it all together. Nice work."

"I'm still not coming back," said Delphine. Roquefort looked disappointed.

"So Mr. Jones has been giving you updates on us," said Kenji. He felt as if he were trying to perform a complex mathematical equation without a calculator. Or paper and pencil.

"He insisted we let you two get the laptop back on your own," said Roquefort.

"That's a big risk to take," said Delphine.

"Does it?" asked Roquefort. "It doesn't sound like you have much confidence in your abilities. We were under the impression the two of you were the best of the best and would have no trouble retrieving a stolen item."

"That part is true, yes," said Kenji. "But I think her concern was for the sensitive information on the laptop."

"Well," said Bing, "we had a kill switch on it. So the data was never actually under threat."

Kenji closed his eyes and tried to wrap his mind around what he was hearing. "You mean…"

"They used us to catch the Solbergs," said Delphine.

Kenji said, "Yes. A clean deal for them, but a messy one for us."

"And all the while we were being babysat by Kapuni Jones," said Delphine.

"Yes," said Kenji. His stomach hurt again.

Roquefort gave Kenji a sharp gaze. "Consider it repayment for having lost the laptop in the first place."

Kenji hung his head. He might have deserved that one.

"But it worked out," said Bing in a peppy tone. "You two are just as clever as we knew you would be." He rubbed his hands together. "Roquefort, I guess we should get back to the bus."

Roquefort shook hands with Kenji and Delphine, and Director Bing did the same.

"Congratulations on your commendation you two, you'll receive a certificate by mail in the next two to six months." Roquefort waved and went down the path.

"Happy retirement," Bing yelled to Kenji. "You're terminated as of today."

CHAPTER 41

The following evening, after a day of much-needed rest, everyone met for dinner to celebrate Marge, Delphine, and Kenji's last night on the island.

"I'm stuffed," said Marge, smoothing the fabric of her jumpsuit over her full tummy. "That was one of the best meals I've ever had!" She probably needed to stop eating such fancy food, or she'd have to buy new jumpsuits soon. Or start exercising. She couldn't decide which option was worse.

"Yes," said Kenji. "Thank you for inviting us all to dinner, Kapuni."

"My pleasure," said Kapuni, beaming. "It was the least I could do after all the excitement we've had."

Marge liked this Kapuni fella. He was awfully charming and obviously had a thing for Delphine. Although Marge couldn't tell if Delphine also had a thing for him; she was hard to read most of the time. But the fact they were all together for dinner must have been a good sign. Marge crossed her fingers under the table—if Delphine had a boyfriend, maybe she'd finally leave her and Kenji alone and not rely on them so much for entertainment.

Griffin and Miko sat across from Marge at the table. Twice already during dinner Marge had accidentally called him

Magnum, but he didn't seem to mind. He and Griffy made a nice couple, and Marge hoped there might be a few sparks there. Her granddaughter deserved to be happy, now she was free from her scuzzy husband. Marge had never liked that Brian guy, but never said anything, trying to respect Griffin's choices. This Hawaiian guy though … Marge approved.

Marge looked around the table. It made her happy to be in such nice company, and currently she felt very satisfied with her life. Kenji took hold of her hand and squeezed it, and her heart swelled.

The sun had set on the other side of the island and the different shades of blue in the bay were fading to black. It was hard to believe just yesterday they'd captured some bad guys. The whole vacation had gone so fast, she almost couldn't believe it. And tomorrow they'd have to leave and go back to Los Angeles.

She'd been staying with Delphine for a few months now, and she wondered how much longer she could manage it. She wouldn't mind permanently moving in and had wanted to talk to Delphine about it. She hadn't worked up her nerve yet.

LA was expensive, and if Marge wanted to stay, she'd have to figure something out, like maybe getting a part time job. Yeah, right! Well, she'd try to enjoy Delphine's generosity for as long as she could. They were family, after all—Delphine couldn't kick her out onto the street. But maybe it wouldn't hurt to have a backup plan.

Their server approached the table with clasped hands. "Are you all ready for your special dessert?" She gave them a pleasant smile.

"We didn't order any dessert," said Delphine.

"I ordered something for the table," said Kenji.

"What are you up to, K-Man?" asked Marge as she nudged his shoulder.

"You will see," he said.

A second server arrived at the table with a rolling cart carrying a large platter of halved pears, a stack of plates, and some shiny metal equipment that looked like it might be a welding rig. He poured a heavy sauce over the pears from a small pitcher.

"Oh, this is really good," said Miko.

"Poached pears with flambéed apricot sauce," said their server.

"Sounds lovely," said Delphine.

The server picked up the small torch from the cart.

"Allow me," said Kenji.

"I'm not supposed to…" said the server.

"It is okay, I am a professional." Kenji stood and gently pried the weapon from her hands. She didn't seem too thrilled about handing over an incendiary device to a guest, but he gave her a look implying he knew what he was doing. Marge was on tenterhooks.

The server took a reluctant step back. Kenji held the torch in one hand and a fancy matching lighter in the other. He sparked the lighter and smiled as he held it to the torch. A huge blue flame shot out of the tip of the torch with an angry intensity.

He turned to the dessert and took a deep breath. With a flourish, he jabbed the torch at the pears and a loud *WHOOSH* pierced the air as the dish of fruit exploded into a fireball, engulfing the cart in flames.

"Whoa, neato!" said Kapuni.

Fortunately, Kenji and the cart were far enough away from the table that the flames stayed contained to the dish of pears. The restaurant must've been prepared for these kinds of mishaps because with a steady hand, the server reached under the cart, pulled out a small fire extinguisher, and wasted no time in spraying that weird, white flame-putting-out stuff all over the pears and Kenji. A thin layer of foam settled on half the table too. Marge was thoroughly impressed.

"In case anyone was wondering," sputtered Kapuni, who had white stuff in his hair and all over his T-shirt, "that's not supposed to happen."

"It did not go quite like I had envisioned," admitted Kenji.

"That's why I never used to let him handle the flame thrower," said Delphine, dusting white particles off her blazer.

Marge appreciated Kenji's grand gesture but would rather have tried the dessert.

"Maybe they can bring us another one," she said hopefully.

"It takes thirty minutes to prepare," said the server, giving Kenji some side-eye.

"It's getting late anyway," said Delphine.

Marge checked her watch. "It's only eight thirty!"

Kenji pulled the server aside and had a whispered conversation with her. Marge couldn't hear what they said, but did catch the words *backup plan*. What was he up to?

He pointed to the club's patio, which their table overlooked. "We will go down there, and Kinsey will bring us decaf coffees and another dessert."

Delphine stood up from the table. "I think I'll go back to my room."

"No!" Kenji shouted. "I mean, please follow me." He left the table and walked down to the pool.

They all shrugged and followed him.

Kenji chose a table near the deep end of the pool, and while they waited for coffee and dessert, Miko wandered off and found something to light a few tiki torches with. He ended up being better with fire than Kenji, and their sitting area was soon illuminated with soft torchlight.

"Kenji Bear, are you okay?" asked Marge. "You're kind of pale and sweaty."

He looked at her with big eyes.

"Are you having a heart attack?" Marge said in a louder voice.

"What?" said Delphine, who had been talking to Kapuni.

Kenji stood up and cleared his throat. He was about to speak when Kinsey and a second server showed up with a tray of coffee cups and a carafe, and a giant sheet cake. Marge peered closely at the cake. The words *HAPPY RETIREMENT, JERRY!* had been written across the top in thick blue icing, and in one corner someone had stuck a hula-girl bobblehead into the cake.

She shot a glance at Delphine, who shook her head; she didn't know what was going on either.

Kenji waited until the servers served everyone coffee and left. He cleared his throat again. "I have an announcement to make."

Everyone waited and stared at him.

"First of all, I want to thank all of you for helping me with the laptop thing. Thanks to you, we saved the computer and caught two criminals. Of course I also got fired, but I am choosing to consider that a good thing."

"Here's to retirement!" said Kapuni. He raised his coffee cup and glanced at the cake.

Everyone raised their cups. "To retirement!"

Then Kenji turned to Marge. "And … I am happy to say I have met the love of my life. Marge, Super Babe, you are the very best, and I am so glad I met you."

Marge blushed and had the presence of mind to stay quiet, although she wanted to start jabbering out of nervousness.

"I cannot imagine spending the rest of my life without you." He knelt in front of her chair and extended his palm, on which rested a small ring box. "Marge Flanders, will you marry me?"

At least two people gasped, but Marge couldn't tell who. One of them might have been her. Her hands flew to her face, and she tried to shut her jaw. It felt wired open with shock. "Oh my goodness," she whispered.

The air felt electric, and no one moved as they waited for her answer.

"I love you too, K-Man, oodles and oodles," she finally said. She felt like she wanted to say something more eloquent, or maybe give a little speech, like Kenji had. But nothing came.

Did she want to get married again? Did she want to spend the rest of her days with one person? And if so, did she want that person to be Kenji Yamamoto?

CHAPTER 42

"Kenji, don't forget to breathe," said Delphine from across the table.

Had he been holding his breath? He gasped for air and realized he had been. He'd asked the love of his life to marry him, and now an eternity had passed and he was still waiting for her answer. Why the hesitation? Was she going to say no? Maybe he needed to sit down. In any case, he should probably stand back up, he thought, so he didn't look like an idiot down on his knees when she declined. He'd be a standing-up idiot.

He got back to his feet and Marge popped out of her chair. "Yes, yes! I will marry you!" She flung her arms around his neck at attacked his face with her delectable lips.

Kapuni clapped. "Yay! I love happy endings!"

"G-ma, I'm so happy for you!" said Griffin.

"Yes, congratulations," said Miko.

Kenji pulled Marge away enough to chance a look at Delphine, who wore a tight smile. "Delphine, do we have your blessing?" he asked in a tentative voice.

Delphine sat with a straight back and to Kenji, she seemed a little sad. Or maybe upset? She hadn't always approved of his and Marge's relationship. A few times Delphine said Marge wasn't good enough for him. Okay, maybe Marge's ex-boyfriend had caused them a little trouble, and perhaps she had a few strange friends, many of whom were named Moe. But his heart wanted what it wanted, and he was prepared to move forward without his best friend's vote of confidence if he had to. He really wanted it though.

"Of course you have my blessing," said Delphine. "Not that you need it."

"You're not just saying that because all these people are here and you're trying to avoid confrontation, are you?" asked Marge.

"No," said Delphine. "I truly want you both to be happy. And if being happy means marriage after less than two months of dating … well, who am I to stand in the way of true love?"

"Okay, great!" said Marge.

"Yes, great," said Kenji with less enthusiasm.

"What about the ring?" asked Griffin, pointing to the box in Kenji's hand.

"Oh yes!" Kenji opened his little ring box. "Marge, this is not your official ring. I bought it in the resort gift shop, and it will have to do until we get home and I can take you shopping."

Nestled inside the box was a small ring made of dark polished wood. "It's koa wood. They told me the tree came from this estate. When it fell, they gave the wood to local craftspeople make little gifts." Kenji carefully slid the ring onto Marge's finger. It fit like it'd been made just for her.

"I love it!" said Marge, and she kissed him on the cheek.

"I will get you a great big diamond once we are back in LA," he said.

Marge extended her arm and viewed the ring from afar. "It's okay K-Man, I think I might have a little something we can use."

"What did you say?" Delphine asked in a higher-than-usual voice.

"Nothing," said Marge. Her face remained expressionless as she looked from Delphine to Griffin.

Griffin frowned. "You don't still have that di—"

"How about we have some dessert?" Delphine said, cutting Griffin off. She pointed to the cake with an overabundance of enthusiasm.

Kapuni laughed. "I have no idea what's going on, but I'm loving all this."

Griffin poured everyone coffee and Kenji, who felt like he'd missed something, cut slices of cake.

"The hula bobblehead is not politically correct," said Kapuni, pointing to the cake. "And who is Jerry?"

Kenji pulled the hula girl off the cake and was about to toss it, but Marge stopped him. "I know it's tacky, but I want it as a memento of this wonderful night. And I think Jerry would want us to have it." She brushed more fire extinguisher foam off Kenji's aloha shirt. Then she gasped. "You don't have any eyebrows!"

"What?" Kenji put down the serving utensils and felt along his brow line. "Huh. I guess they got burned off in the pear explosion."

Griffin squinted at him. "Yup, you're naked up there."

"Oh well," said Kenji. "I guess that will be my memento of this wonderful evening."

"I'm all for mementos, but I do kinda hope they grow back," said Marge. "Your eyebrows were very sexy."

Cake was served, and they all sat around the little table enjoying Jerry's retirement dessert. When Kinsey had told Kenji the only other special dessert they had left was an unclaimed cake for a canceled party, he'd jumped on it, but now he felt a little bad for Jerry, whoever he was, and wondered why the poor fellow didn't end up getting his retirement celebration.

CHAPTER 43

"Now you're engaged, maybe you'd like to stay with your fiancé for our last night here in Hawaii," Delphine said to Marge as they ate their cake. Delphine wouldn't be able to forgive herself if she didn't try one more time to get Marge out of her room.

"No, I don't think so," said Marge. "I mean, you and me are roomies, Big D! I wouldn't want you to get lonely."

"How many times do I have to tell you that's impossible?" Delphine said. She couldn't believe she'd only gotten one night to herself in her beautiful suite.

Marge put her plate down. "I'm sorry. I really thought it would be okay to hook up with Kenji here, but I guess I'm not ready yet."

"But you're ready to marry him," said Delphine.

"Uh-huh, well, people are weird, aren't they," snapped Marge. "I'm sure by the time we plan the wedding and everything, I'll be ready. We'll plan a long engagement."

"I'm sorry," said Delphine.

"For what?"

"I actually respect your point of view quite a lot. I suppose I'm just being grouchy."

Marge leaned over in her chair and gave Delphine a hug. "Oh Big D, you're such a good pal."

Delphine wondered if maybe Kenji's dessert explosion might be a bad omen for the couple's upcoming nuptials. How could anyone get married after knowing the other person for only a few months? It seemed awfully reckless. Especially when one of the people involved was Marge.

When everyone had gotten their fill of Jerry's cake, Miko and Griffin excused themselves, promising to be in front of the hotel lobby first thing in the morning to take the travelers to the airport in one of the shuttle vans. Not long after, Kenji and Marge decided to go dancing. One last night on the town, they said. Marge asked Delphine if she wanted to go, but of course she did not. Kapuni didn't want to go either; he stayed seated at the table when Marge and Kenji left.

"You wanna walk?" Kapuni asked, hopping to his feet.

"That would be nice." Delphine stood and they strolled down the path to the beach. Where the path met the sand, Delphine took off her shoes and put them under a nearby tree. Of course Kapuni wasn't wearing any to begin with.

A few people sat in chairs along the sand, and two kids played in the shallow water.

"So what do you think about your friends getting married?" asked Kapuni.

"Well…"

"Let me guess. You don't want to say anything bad, so you won't say anything at all."

"I might say something eventually, but not right now. They're both so happy."

"Why say anything?" he asked.

"They hardly know each other," said Delphine. "How can they know they want to spend the rest of their lives together? And you don't know Marge like I do. That one's trouble."

"Phooey," said Kapuni. "Maybe Kenji wants some trouble. Some good trouble!"

Delphine wasn't convinced Marge was "good trouble," but it wasn't worth arguing about.

They continued down the beach. The sand felt cool on the bottoms of Delphine's feet. The evening was quiet; she felt heartbroken about leaving such a lovely place.

"You owe me an apology," said Kapuni after they'd walked a few more minutes.

"I can't imagine what for."

Kapuni adjusted his Dodgers hat. "You accused me not only of stealing your friend's laptop, but of trying to sink my nephew's friend's boat, with you on it."

"Oh, right," said Delphine.

"Well?" His eyebrows rose.

"I'm not sure I am sorry."

"Phooey," said Kapuni.

"Look, we don't know each other," said Delphine. "And I don't trust you. I saw you talking to Minka and Martin the other day."

"But I'm also chummy with Kenji's boss, doesn't that count for something?"

"It means you could be a double agent of some kind."

Kapuni tilted his head in thought. "Okay, I guess I see your point. But everything with me is on the up and up! At least for the most part. And if it makes you feel any better, I don't trust you either."

"Why on earth not?" Delphine felt affronted.

"Okay fine, I trust you. I was just saying that."

They got to the water's edge and turned up the beach in the opposite direction they'd gone when he'd taken her for fish tacos. She wished she could've gone there again before she had to leave.

"Do you really work for the Falls?" she asked.

They waded into the water up to their ankles as they walked.

"I did," he said, sounding more serious. "Way back when. We kind of had a falling out, but I am still in touch with certain people."

"Your name wasn't in any of the databases," said Delphine.

"That is a story for another day doesn't it! But there is something else."

Dread sat in her stomach, right on top of the cake.

"I knew your husband Charles long ago."

Delphine stopped walking. She felt cold all of a sudden, like an arctic wind had replaced the tropical breeze.

"How?" was all she could get out.

"We were friends before he met you. Well, I should say we worked together. A long time ago."

"He never mentioned you, I'd have remembered," she said.

"I bet you didn't—or couldn't tell him everything either."

Delphine just nodded. That was definitely true. They didn't talk about work much, but they'd always talked about the important things. Their children, their relationship. How they'd felt about each other. A twinge of sadness ran through her chest.

"I always kept track of him. And then he passed away..." Kapuni sighed. "I am sorry for your loss."

"Thank you," said Delphine.

"When Fausto mentioned his friend Delphine Lougheed was coming for a visit, naturally I was curious. What kind of woman could have captivated Charles? And Fausto, for that matter? I had to meet you. And you are so enchanting! I can see why both men were in love with you."

"That's very flattering, I suppose." Delphine felt like she might hit overwhelm at any second. He'd known her darling Charles! She had so many questions about the past, but didn't know where to start.

She cleared her throat and tried to shift back to the present situation. "Why were you talking to Minka and Martin at the pool?" she asked. "And before you give me some smarty-pants answer, I suggest you tell me the complete truth. Otherwise there is no point in us remaining friends."

They started down the beach again.

"Are we really friends?" he asked.

Delphine didn't answer.

"Okay, here's the deal," said Kapuni. "I was trying to find out why the Solbergs were in Hawaii. I may have mentioned I have a lot of connections on the island—which is totally true, by the way—and they asked me if I knew anything about local pineapple farming."

"Hmm," said Delphine. "That's odd."

"Eh, maybe," said Kapuni. "But the next night, when we went to the bungalows, it all made sense."

"How so?"

"The guy who answered the door. The Samoan? His name is Sandy Kainalu. He and his brother Salomon are known locally as the Pineapple Brahs."

"Let me guess," said Delphine. "A pineapple mafia?"

"Ha-ha, pineapple mafia! But yes. My guess is the Solbergs were trying to diversify from fish into fruit."

"That must be why they wanted money—to buy their way in. Who wouldn't want to trade the cold climate of Norway for this?" She looked out at the water.

"I love Kaimoa Bay," said Kapuni. "I'm glad you like it."

"This might be one of the nicest places I've visited," she admitted.

"But you didn't get to see much of the real charm of Mokumoa, cooped up at the resort. This is not the real Hawaii."

"I know," said Delphine. "It's been very lovely, and quite luxurious, but the place feels isolating. It would be nice to see other parts of the island. Maybe I'll have to come back."

"You should!" said Kapuni.

Delphine stopped walking and gazed up at the sky. Kapuni waded farther out into the water and splashed his feet around. Here under the moon and in front of the beautiful bay, she had the courage to admit she enjoyed spending time with Kapuni. He was funny and smart. And a little weird, sure, but being serious all the time was overrated. Oh my, she thought. She'd learned that from living with Marge.

She had so many questions! And so much to think about. Kapuni had known Charles and had been watching out for her during her stay on the island. Part of her felt resentful Kapuni had assumed she needed looking after. Another part of her was flattered.

Kapuni waded back onto the shore, and they started walking back to the resort.

"This vacation didn't really turn out like I'd hoped," said Delphine.

"No? Oh, you mean it turned out way better than you hoped," said Kapuni.

"All I wanted was some peace and quiet. Some time to myself."

Kapuni laughed. "I don't think so! Let's face it, you didn't really want a boring vacation. You wanted distractions. Why do you think all this craziness manifested?" He waved his arms around.

Oh dear, thought Delphine. Apparently he was one of those people who used the word *manifest*.

"Anyway, I just have one regret about your visit," he said, now sounding more somber.

"What's that?"

"I didn't get to take you out on a date."

"I'm not sure I trust you enough to go out on a date with you anyway," said Delphine.

"I respectfully have to disagree," said Kapuni. "You not only trust me, you also like me."

"Well," said Delphine, "I don't know." But she did know.

"Phooey!" said Kapuni.

The moon came out overhead and bathed them in a silvery glow.

"Come on," he said. "Not knowing how things will go is what makes life so fun. If you think about it, a little bit of mystery is the perfect way to start what could be a really nice friendship," said Kapuni.

Delphine thought about it. "I believe you're right."

NEXT IN THE SERIES

Be the first to know about upcoming new releases, including the next installment of the Old School Mystery series

Sign up for the AceWrites newsletter to stay in the loop!
acneil.com/newsletter

BOOKS BY ANDREA C. NEIL

OLD SCHOOL MYSTERIES

The Blingsters

The Big Cheese

Gone Grandpa

The Last Resort

THE BEVERLEY GREEN ADVENTURES

Beverley Green's First Adventure

Beverley Green's First Territorial Christmas

Beverley Green Finds True North

Beverley Green Comes Home

The Guthrie Short Stories

MICRO FICTION

Days Are Beautiful: 100 flash fiction stories

No Surprises: 100 flash fiction stories

Visit acneil.com for more information

ACKNOWLEDGMENTS

The inspiration for Kaimoa Bay is a real place, and I have real friends who are real nice about letting me come stay there. I sit on their balcony all day drinking Spindrift and watching the water change colors. So a very big thank you to Dayl, Russ, and their dog Hallie for letting me stay in paradise! It has soothed my soul more than you can ever know.

Thanks to Karen Bates for the cover art and being my very best email friend. We met online in 2006, when she had a blog for her artwork and I had some weird blog called "Ambitious Hamster" where I prattled on like I usually do. Thanks Ren, for everything.

Thanks to Michele Chiappetta for being the voice of editing reason, thanks to my family for sometimes admitting to be related to me, and thanks to Marcus for making dinner and washing so many dishes so I could finish this dang book.

Thanks to my ARC readers and a super-duper, ahoy-matey thanks to YOU!

-ace

ABOUT THE AUTHOR

Andrea lives in Oklahoma but grew up in Southern California—
and the latter will always be home in her heart. In 2015 she left a
job in finance to follow her passion for writing and creating art.
With age comes wisdom, or at least a few more stories to tell, and
in 2018, Andrea began self-publishing quirky novels with the
intention of brightening her readers' day. When she's not trying to
get her own words onto a page, Andrea edits other people's
writing, eats dark chocolate, and goes on walks if the weather's
nice.

acneil.com

amazon.com/author/andreaneil
bookbub.com/profile/andrea-c-neil
facebook.com/andreacneil
instagram.com/andreacneil